HARLEQUINADE

Harlequinade

Fifteen Short Stories

Lindsay Pritchard

Richmond Pickering Ltd

First published in Great Britain 2013
by Richmond Pickering Ltd
Denmark Cottage
Lower Hengoed
Oswestry
Shropshire SY10 7EF

www.richmondpickering.com

British Library Cataloguing-in-Publication Data
A catalogue record for this book is available from the British Library

All of the characters in this book are fictitious and any resemblance to actual persons, living or dead, is purely coincidental.

Cover design by Rose Kidson

ISBN-10: 0957237243
ISBN-13: 978-0-9572372-4-7

Dedication

William, George and Mary

Acknowledgements

With grateful acknowledgements to Sue Johnson for applying some literary polish to some fairly rough scripts. And also to Rebecca Richmond and Claire Pickering of Richmond Pickering Ltd for their advice and encouragement in helping me fulfil a lifelong ambition. And, to you, the reader – I hope you get as much enjoyment from reading these stories as I did in writing them.

Contents

Foreword

"Sit up and pay attention there! Yes, I do mean you! Now, I know how these things work. I've vast experience of picking up books. You look at the cover. If sufficiently impressed, you have a butcher's at the back cover and check out what *Rat Catcher Monthly* and *The Crochet Gazette* have had to say about it:

> I will waste no time in reading this book.

> Like a faithful dog, I could not put it down.

Or some other such confection. But, eventually, you commit your pocket money and take it home. And then you read it.

If you liked it, you might just glimpse the author blurb. Then – last of all – you will read the foreword.

Am I right?

If you've done it the conventional way – front to back – then well done you, but you need therapy for your anal personality. As for the rest of us, we're all wondering idly why there is a foreword by the author at all. That's assuming we haven't been able to get Barack Obama or Thierry Henry or Stephen Fry (although he's everywhere else) to endorse it.

Let me explain my theory. It's a five-minute soapbox which you'll just have to sit and listen to while you relax there in your Ladybird winceyettes (the ones with the ladybird lookalike buttons) and sip your posset of choice.

First, in praise of the short story. Sometimes you just need a cheeseburger and a coke, not a full cordon-bleu meal with an imposing little Château Pétrus 1961. Something you can snack on when on the train or at your desk or maybe just a quickie before lights out (don't go there, you're just getting smutty now).

And instead of following 320 pages of Daphne who has a crisis with the Aga amidst the longueurs of her existential ennui, you get to meet at least fifteen characters who might entertain you, make you think, surprise you or maybe – just briefly – touch your heart.

Secondly, it's a much underrated sport. It can take almost as much time to craft a short story as a novel. There is a famous apology attributed – variously – to Blaise Pascal, Mark Twain, Oscar Wilde and Voltaire, amongst others, which goes:

> I'm sorry this is so long. I didn't have time to make it shorter.

Or maybe you prefer Hawkeye from *M*A*S*H*:

> If you bring that sentence in for a fitting I can
> have it shortened by Wednesday.

Remember those exercises at school where you had to précis some long-winded passage or other? Well, they don't do that any more – they're all focusing on making inclusive dinosaurs out of toilet rolls.

Anyway, a short story should be a précis of a novel. But a novelist is allowed to take flights of fancy, introduce extraneous characters or simply indulge in a stream of consciousness. And you allow a degree of tolerance while you decide if you can "get into it". Not allowed for a short story writer.

If you've not been grabbed by paragraph two then you're off. The short story writer says:

> Grab them by the tentacles (sic) and their
> hearts and minds will surely follow.

And that can be tough to do. But there is a great literary tradition – look them up on Wikipedia, there's millions of them – who demonstrate the point: H. G. Wells; P. G. Wodehouse; William Trevor; Roald Dahl. Not that I'm bracketing myself among such luminaries, but you get the point. It may be short, but look how it does it for you.

Perhaps you have heard that said before in some different context?

Thirdly (and lastly – I can feel you dropping off) can I attempt to answer the question: "Where do the ideas come from?"

Well, I think it helps to live a little first. There is a rich tableau out there. A cast of characters, a Harlequinade of people, and everyone has a story to tell.

Sorry if I offend you but sci-fi, magic worlds and invented kingdoms have nothing on real-life 24-carat heroes. Experiencing different cultures and geographies help. But some of these stories just come from listening to the news and thinking: What if …?

So do try this at home folks, if you want to join in. Instead of Googling recipes for ox liver, the Lake District Pencil Museum or cute pictures of cats in deely boppers, just sit there.

Chew the end of your pencil and get into the zone. It's OK, too, if you want to do it in your yoga class. Let your brain go for a walk and see where it takes you.

Join us. You might like it. Some of the stories in this book come from such enforced idleness.

I hope you enjoy them.

Now ... lights out.

A Very Small Life

What do you know about the term "Persistent Vegetative State"? He had been ushered into a cubicle-sized room, reduced in size even more by shelves stacked with files and textbooks with complicated titles.

Opposite him sat a small, middle-aged woman with the accoutrements of medical identification – white coat, stethoscope, a small square badge with the name "Dr Hewitt Consultant" on it and a studied concerned air. Her accent was – what? South African? Australian? He couldn't place it. No matter.

She addressed him whilst consulting her computer screen.

'Well … I've heard of it. Something to do with being brain-dead?' he ventured quizzically.

'That's a useful layman's handle but medically not quite correct,' she advised, looking importantly over her half-rimmed reading glasses. 'In fact, the brainstem – or reptile brain as we sometimes call it for shorthand – is functioning. This means there can be some residual reflex brain activity, but the cerebral cortex – the bit of brain that lets us think – is just not working.

'Patients do vary, but after a period of time in this stage, say nine to twelve months, and when we're not registering anything on an MRI or PET scan in the thinking areas, it's pretty safe to say that there is no thinking going on any more. More important, it suggests that the chances of recovery are pretty much nil. That's where we are with your father.'

He pulled a deferential "that's important medical stuff I didn't know" face.

'I haven't seen him for – oh, years. How did he get into this state, anyway?'

She continued her mini-lecture, factual, dispassionate and mildly medically patronising.

'With your father it was a vascular intracranial haemorrhage. A stroke, if you like. The episode was so massive that it completely knocked out any cognitive functions. We've done regular tests. The neurologists all agree they can't find any cerebral activity. We continue to provide nutrition and hydration, but after a year or so and at his age, we begin to consider whether it is sound medicine or, indeed' – she searched for the word – 'a kindness to keep him in this state.'

'So this is where I come in, I suppose. By the way, how did you find me? I haven't had anything to do with him since I was small.'

'Oh, we have our ways,' she said conspiratorially. 'Social services records, National Insurance, various registers and so on.' She squinted at the computer. 'It says that his wife – your mother, I suppose – divorced him, moved up to Lancashire in the 1970s, but died about five years ago. Oh, I hope you knew about that?'

'Yes,' he agreed. 'Didn't have much to do with her, either. Broken home – three of us boys all scattered to the winds. Lost touch with the others. We were very young; moved about a lot. Maybe they are abroad. Who knows?'

Mini-lifetime stories of three lost boys, distilled into a single, short paragraph.

She continued without any requisite regrets or any compassionate reflection.

'Well, we've reached the stage where decisions must be made. Usually there's an obvious next of kin, but in the final analysis we make an application to the courts. Fortunately, in this case we did a final search and it turned you up.'

He reflected on the word "fortunately", eyes askance.

'My job is to give you all the facts and help facilitate a decision. If you do decide on a non-interventionist approach, we will give you all the background you need.'

'What do you mean by "non-interventionist"?'

'By that we mean the withdrawal of support, whether that be food, water or medication. Expiry can be a matter of hours or – at worst – days. Since there is no cognitive awareness, there is no pain or distress to the patient. I have been involved in many similar cases and there is simply a cessation of life.'

'Death, you mean?'

'It all depends on your philosophical analysis of the term "death",' she corrected. 'If the person cannot think, move, experience emotions, walk, talk and so on, then the experts would say there is no death in the accepted sense.'

He mused briefly on the semantics but did not feel qualified to argue with this experienced viewpoint.

'So what happens next?'

'You will no doubt want to see him and we will give you all the time you need to arrive at your decision. We will respect your wishes, but I am sure you will conclude, given the circumstances, that active non-intervention' – he struggled again with the semantics – 'is the best way to proceed forall concerned.

'Let me assure you that all the tests we have done show beyond any reasonable doubt that there is no thinking or emotions apparent. PVS patients can sometimes react to certain stimuli. They can even move or make noises. But in no sense can this be linked with higher brain activity. Anyway, let's go and see him and we'll leave you alone for whatever time you need. Then there will be some paperwork to complete should you decide that our advice is the appropriate course of action.'

They both rose from their chairs.

'Thank you,' he said.

Outside the office, she introduced him to Rose, a brisk, smiling nurse who was deputed to take him along to the side ward.

'You must be feeling pretty bad,' she said with a smiling Irish lilt and a compassionate hand on his arm.

'I'm OK,' he said, with a shake of his head. 'We weren't very close. In fact, it must be forty or fifty years since I last had anything to do with him.'

Rose gave an understanding nod and said, 'Nevertheless, it's often quite hard to take. Seeing people ill can be painful. But looking at them and seeing nothing apparently wrong can be very unsettling. They make no reaction when you speak to them or touch them.

'But don't let me put you off. The science is all very well, but I get my nurses to treat them like human beings. Who knows what might be going on in there? Anyway, just a word of warning, you might find all the drips, tubes and monitors a bit of a shock.'

Rose opened the door of a side ward and strode into a dimly lit room containing a bed, a locker, a small table with various medical receptacles, some monitors and a chair.

'Here we are, Albert, 'she said breezily, 'a visitor. We can't remember one of those before, can we? It's your son, Stanley, come to see you.' All said with a loud, Joyce Grenfell inflection. 'Well, I'll leave you with him, Stanley, and if there's anything you need, just push that buzzer there and I'll pop down. Can I get you a cup of tea to be going on with?'

'No thanks, Rose, I'm fine.'

Rose left and closed the door. He looked around. It was a dismal, bland room. A drip. A chart headed "Albert Arthur Maybury. DOB 1/9/1930". The chart had numbers, hieroglyphics, times, dates, observations, signatures, that were all indecipherable to him. A single window overlooked a car park and beyond, to a cluster of factory buildings.

On the bed was a figure in a sepulchral position. Eyes closed, immobile. The only sign of life was the monitor which emitted a slow, steady bleep and displayed some numbers – blood pressure and heart rate, he supposed.

He walked past the chair, glancing at the figure, but then looked out of the window to reflect on the situation.

Outside, a bright, still, early November day was drawing to a close. The sun had already disappeared behind the buildings. A plume of smoke hung in the air a distance away. He thought about how he had come to be here. An unexpected telephone call with brief, but startling, news. The basic factual details. A request. Booking a half-day off work. Many years had gone by. A lot of time. A lot of water under a lot of bridges. Still a residual anger.

He sat down on the spartan chair next to the figure in bed.

'Well, Albert Arthur Maybury,' he said, reading the name off the patient's chart. 'Believe it or not, it's one of your forgotten offspring, Stanley, here. Apparently with the power to decide if we pull the plug or not. Can't think of many reasons why we shouldn't, can you?'

He wasn't sure why he was speaking his thoughts out loud, but it just felt fairer to articulate what he was thinking, given the gravity of his responsibility. He folded his arms, looked at the figure and shook his head.

'I don't suppose for a minute you give a damn about what's happened in my life, but since I've got the chance, and since I have your full attention, I might as well sound off for a bit.'

He leaned forward and rested his arms on the regulation white sheet and light blue hospital blanket.

'Mr Copestake, the social worker, let me read the file some years ago. I was curious and insisted on my rights. The year was 1957 and we were whisked away by the social under something called a Place of Safety Order. You spent all your dole down at the local, lowering pints of Watneys, smoking and playing cribbage.

'Apparently, you interrupted this industrious life from time to time to wander home, beat up the wife and clatter us kids if we got in the way of any of your indulgences. We were dirty, undernourished and scared. So it seemed a good idea to put is in care. Only "care" didn't cover keeping us together, it seemed.

'I didn't see the other two until we were rounded up one day and put into Brampton Place. "The Orphanage", it was called. Well, we might as well have been orphans. Do you know what? It was such a Gothic monstrosity. Near the entrance was a big cage for two enormous Airedale dogs. Eric started crying because he thought we were being put in prison.

'No – "care" meant keeping us fed and watered, and making sure that any physical chastisement was below the radar for formal action. I'm sure it's a bit better today.'

He looked out of the window at the darkening sky and remembered Mr Stubbs and his visits to the boys' communal bedroom. Mrs Rampley, the matron, with her cane. Time spent on "jankers" for crimes and misdemeanours, involving working in the kitchens or polishing the Big Hall and stairs for minor infractions of pointless rules.

'From time to time, people "borrowed" us for the weekend. I guess it was the early version of fostering. Most of them weren't much interested in you, but I suppose there was money in it for them at that time. But I tried my best. I wanted to be claimed by someone. I was like one of those weeds that you see hanging onto a wall, with no visible reason why they should be growing there. I wanted to be part of a family unit. Any, really. Then there was the drive back to Brampton Place on the Monday, in Mr Copestake's car. You always wondered why they didn't want to see you again.'

He addressed the recumbent figure more directly.

'And what were you doing all this time, Albert Arthur? Down the pub, on the pop – and never a backward glance. If you could register this, I hope you would feel ashamed. But you can't and here you are, still blissfully ignorant.

'Anyway, I made my mind up from an early age that I had two roads to choose from and I had to take the positive one. Otherwise, I'd have been a delinquent or followed you down the pub, or maybe into drugs, or ended up in prison, or wrapped round a tree, or even blown my brains out.

'But I decided to make a go of it. Knuckled down, got a few O levels. Left care at fifteen, and got some paying lodgings and an apprenticeship. Stayed out of trouble and kept my nose clean.

'Are you listening to this, Albert? No thanks at all to you. And all this time, all these people you were responsible for bringing into the world were collateral damage. But I told myself it was up to me to grow up fast. You know what? I've come through it.'

He reflected silently for a while on the oppressive care home regime. The miserable Monday drive back. Then, tantalisingly, there had been times when he felt he had a place in the sun. Sitting in the Stanhopes' lounge on a Saturday evening with a round of ham sandwiches, some squash and *Dixon of Dock Green* on the telly.

He thought about his supervisor at the factory, Tommy Wheeler. He'd thought he was a hard bastard at first, but he was always there for him, with some patient advice and homespun philosophy, in those early, impressionable years. Just now and then there was a place in the sun. And he kept these memories, burnished regularly.

'Yeah, head down, bum up. That was me. Paid my way and sorted myself out. Kept out of trouble. I said to myself, if I ever had my own family, I wouldn't piss the chance up against the wall like Albert Arthur Maybury did.'

Then he thought about something and a quiet smile spread over his face.

'But you know what was the best thing that happened to me? Made up for a lot of the shit that went before. Meeting Pamela. I should tell you about her. She worked in the offices at Bargrove & Fennell. Secretary. Nothing fancy. Never really noticed her at first. She wasn't the forward type and, to tell you the truth, not much of a looker. She'd had a scalding accident when she was young and got some scars on her. So she wasn't what I thought of as girlfriend material.

'But the night I got talking to her accidentally at the Xmas do was just the start of the rest of my life. We never looked back, even though I know I tested her patience at times. I called her The Klingon because I couldn't get rid of her. Tell you the truth, after a while I realised I never would want to because she was my anchor.

'You would have liked her. An unpolished gem. She was my wingman. Looked after my back. She would take a bullet for me. And a hard worker. Jeeze! When I got made redundant for a while, The Klingon didn't moan. She got two jobs. Worked in a pub and did some early morning cleaning. We got through it. We haven't got much but we don't need much. Council house. No debts. Crappy old car. A week every year in a caravan in Criccieth. We've got everything we need and I've got the family I always wanted.'

There was a knock at the door. Rose looked in.

'Anything you want, Stanley? Tea? Coffee? Sandwich? I heard you talking. That's good. You never know, you know.'

He demurred, politely, and told Rose that, yes, he was putting a few things straight. It was probably going in one ear and out the other, but at least he was getting things off his chest, and it made him feel better, anyway.

'Well, I'll leave you to it. Give me a shout if there's anything you need,' said Rose, disappearing with a friendly smile.

He addressed the sarcophagus again.

'She seems to think you might be registering some of this, you old sod. Well, how things turned out with me and how I never let your neglect grind me down. In fact, I've used it to make something of my life, however humdrum it's been.

'I know I was never a genius or fated to make a lot of money, but I've got on with it. Just trying to be a good family man. Good worker. Good bloke.

'You also need to know about Michael. He's your grandson. You know; the one you never met. It was a struggle to have him. The Klingon had a hard time having him and that put paid to the idea of any more kids. He grew up secure, knowing his dad and mum loved him. That's probably what turned him into such a great lad. Never an ounce of bother with him. Stayed out of trouble. Got through school and got himself a job. Good-looking lad, as well. No idea where he got that from.'

He chuckled to himself.

'Michael never needed "stuff", like all his mates. And if he went through a rebel stage, he did it very quietly and never announced it. A great kid.'

Stanley stood up and looked out of the window, watching the light fading and the late afternoon traffic moving slowly in a melee of traffic lights, indicators and headlights. He felt a film over his eyes.

'But you'll never see him now. We lost him last year. His mate Paul was giving him a lift back from work on his motorbike. Some white van man came round the corner on the wrong side of the road. Suspended sentence and a £750 fine for careless driving, he got. We lost a smashing lad forever. Pamela was devastated. Seemed to be in a trance for weeks. Couldn't get through to her.'

He stopped to think deep thoughts and sighed heavily.

'You missed all this, didn't you? And you'll never know what a fine young man he was. Not that you would have bothered, anyway,' he said, with anger in his voice.

He sat down again, composing himself. He fancied that the figure in the bed gave several deep breaths. Just the reptile brain keeping him functioning, he thought.

'Anyway, she'll never be the same. It'll never get any easier. But we just said we were lucky to have him for nineteen great years, and he will have wanted us to get on with life. Sometimes, when it gets all too black, I can almost hear him saying that.

'So we do get on with it. There are times now when we can smile and even some days when we don't mention him at all. Although he's always there.

'The Klingon does the house and I get on with my work and our life. It's a very small life, I grant you, but we have to make the best of what we've got.

'So here I am, just trying to make my way in this mad world. I'm no saint, by any means, but I rub along, usually trying to do the decent thing.

'Where's it all going, though? I was at work recently. I looked up at the clock and suddenly realised I was fifty-eight. Bit of a slap in the face when you suddenly see time passing like that. But I look back and ask myself, would I have done anything different? And I can honestly say no. I've tried to look after the family, work hard, stay positive.' He looked at the reclining figure. 'And what would you say, Albert, if you asked yourself that question? All the things you missed just so you could get another pint down you. It's how you'll be remembered by other people that's important in life. And who's going to remember you? Maybe the landlord at The Crown.'

He put his folded arms on the bed and rested his head on them. He stayed that way for fully five minutes, then slowly sat back in the chair.

'But life isn't fair, is it?' he asked in a soft whisper. 'Here you are. Never done a tap in your life, created mayhem and havoc. Shirked all your responsibilities and just pleased yourself. Now you've got a free bed, all the mod cons that the state can provide to keep you going until you slip quietly and painlessly away, off into oblivion. You don't know how lucky you are.'

He thought for a while and then frowned as though a sudden pain had hit him.

'Pamela's got it, you know. I think it was the shock of Michael that triggered it off. Quacks say it's one of the bad ones. Secondaries. We're talking months, not years. You know what she said when we came out of the specialist's office? She said, "I'm really, really sorry, Stanley. I'm going to be leaving you on your own. I'm going to fight it as long as I can."'

He folded his arms and sobbed quietly.

'That's the type of person she is. Always thinking of others. I've no idea what it's going to be like when she's gone. But I'll have to try to stay positive like I've had to do before. Otherwise, it's going to be a very black place.' He addressed the recumbent figure. 'Maybe you're in a black place, too. It would only be justice.'

His face softened.

'But do you remember that day you came to get me out of the home for an afternoon out? You must have been having one of your sober moments. Hot June day, it was. We went to the fair. You bought me a set of skittles from the shops. Do you remember buying me a Knickerbocker Glory? You said it was nearly as big as me. Then you gave me a piggyback to the home. You won't remember it, but I do. Just for one day you were my dad. I've stored it away. I think about it now and then. Never really told anybody.'

He reached out and held the lifeless hand.

'You see, part of it is being able to forgive and move on. See the good in people and try to disregard all the badness. Whatever you did or didn't do, that day told me there *was* some good in you, somewhere deep down. Whatever happened, happened. You were still my dad. And now I'll try to do the right thing for you.'

He sat there for a while, immobile. Then, almost imperceptibly, he felt the hand move slowly and the fingers weakly encircled his hand. He looked in astonishment. The hand lightly gripped his.

His mind took a while to register this. Then he remembered that patients in this state could react or move or make a noise. This was nothing significant. He looked at the figure's face as if to confirm the lack of consciousness.

What he saw startled him.

A tear trickled out of the corners of both eyes and down over the sunken cheeks. He jumped up and rang the bell. After a short while, Rose came cheerily in.

'All done, Stanley?' she inquired. 'Do you want to pop in and see Doctor Hewitt and sign it all off?'

He could hardly get the words out.

'No,' he said. 'That's the last thing I'm going to do.'

A Good Lawyer

What's the best way to get down to Wall Street? They're signing the Pereira deal and I have to watch that those sharks from Atlanta haven't slipped some doozies into the contract. I hear there's hold-ups?'

Marjorie, as always, looking crisp in her discreet black-and-white motif executive secretary clothes, gave him a staccato summary.

'Crane collapse on Forty-eighth and Fifth. A police gun incident has gridlocked Broadway to Eighth. And the subway is only intermittent because of driver action.'

'Inaction,' he corrected. 'Well, how the hell do I get down there?' he asked beseechingly.

'Oh, and I forgot, it's the Macy's Thanksgiving Day parade, too,' Marjorie grimaced apologetically.

'I can only suggest you take your chances on the subway. Shall I ring and tell Mortlocks to hold until you get there?'

'Yes, yes. What the hell is happening to this city?'

Jackson Shucksmith, legal principal of Shucksmith & Schuster, was not accustomed to having to negotiate such inconsequential detail. Didn't all these people realise the commercial significance of this meeting? Millions of dollars, thousands of jobs, complex financing – not to mention the gargantuan egos of the two big, swinging dicks involved.

Oh, and legal fees – now topping seven figures for this one – helping to swell the Shucksmith & Schuster bonus pool. And boy, did he need that bonus! Vanessa was, even now, closing on the holiday home in The Hamptons. The schooling fees for the two boys were more than a hundred big ones. The exclusive Upper East Side apartment ran out at £10k a month. Shirts from Bergdorf Goodman; shoes from Crockett & Jones; suits tailor-made by Borrello himself; Vanessa's expensive home-furnishing tastes. Then, of course, the membership fees for the Yale Club and the Algonquin, fencing lessons at the Health and Racquets Club – hell, those were a normal family's budget.

No, looking good and living high certainly soaked up lots of greenbacks. As well that the partnership was pre-eminent.

Jack Welch once said, 'If you want a lawyer, get a phone book. If you want a deal, get Shucksmith.'

Some three generations had cemented their place in US commercial life. If you had to ask the price, you were in the wrong office. S & S didn't give you any itemised bill – just a big number on an invoice marked "For Services Rendered".

People paid because they knew. If you needed to be sure. If you wanted to intimidate. If you wanted to avoid the elephant traps, then the discreet door off Columbus was where you went.

People paid because the partners' mahogany desks, panelled walls, fine art, thick carpets and antique clocks soothed and reassured. And people paid because Jackson Shucksmith was The Man.

And The Man was looking zingy today; trademark blue pinstripe; signature silk handkerchief; two-hundred-dollar haircut. He adjusted the Henri Bendel tie in the gilt mirror in the lobby and nodded approvingly at himself as he smoothed his hair.

Even without the fetching ensemble, he would have cut an impressive figure. Well above average height, with a handsome, pleasingly contoured face under dark hair, with just a fleck or two of grey for gravitas. Laser blue eyes that he used to charm or to fix and skewer lesser counsel. Add to this an attractive dark voice with just a hint of patrician "creak". Plus an innate ability to assimilate facts, sift, weigh and mentally summarise key points before delivering exquisitely argued and watertight opinions. When Jackson Shucksmith spoke, others stopped, listened and admired.

It was helpful, too, that he had the survival instincts of a piranha.

Just now, though, there was the irksome business of public transport. The subway steps were thronged with New Yorkers trying to get across town. There was a long queue for the ticket machine and Jackson cursed silently. He consulted his Audemars Piguet timepiece – so very much more discreet than a nouveau riche Rolex – and pulled a face. He hoped Marjorie had stroked the client with sufficient unction.

Beyond the press and before the turnstile was a half-sized billboard warning of subway disruption. Near it stood a grey-haired black man speaking to each individual as they passed through. Panhandling. The mayor really needed to get a grip on these people. Get them out of the city, flush them out of the subway and let people go about their lawful business unmolested. He fumed whilst a gang of teenage skateboarders held a debate amongst themselves about payment. Finally, he inserted his platinum card and secured his ticket. He didn't carry cash. You couldn't be too sure.

Approaching the turnstile, he sensed the black guy trying to catch his attention. But Jackson knew the rules. No eye contact. Preserve an air of professional detachment. Then he made an elementary mistake. He locked eyes.

'Sir,' said an old voice. 'Please, sir, I just need to get through.'

Jackson closed his eyes and gave a quizzical half turn of the head as though a witness's answer had been diffidently rebuffed.

'And how am I supposed to help?'

'You can just let me squeeze through with you.'

'Why would I?'

'I ain't got no money for no fare and I just need to get home.'

Jackson quickly computed the permutations. Best to ignore him. This was, after all, an illegal conspiracy. Suppose there were CCTV cameras. He would be identified, prosecuted, disgraced and drummed out of the profession. And, in any case, why would he want this dirty old hobo, obviously a no-hoper, sharing a narrow turnstile with him and mussing up his outfit?

He looked at the man again. Old, lined, slightly bent over. Clothes probably recovered from a dumpster.

The old man looked at the smart businessman with the air of a hesitant animal waiting to be disciplined.

Then Jackson did something uncharacteristic. Something he would later consider so off-piste that he couldn't figure where the impulse had come from.

'OK. Come on – but be quick.'

He swiped his ticket and the old man squeezed through with him.

'Thank you, sir. Thank you, sir. God bless you, sir.'

He dismissed the thanks briskly, with closed eyes and a benevolent don't-mention-it shake of the head. Then the man was gone amongst the crowd waiting for the delayed train.

Jackson stood for a while in thought. He looked at his shoes and pondered for a long couple of minutes. Then, with an uncomprehending face, he went to look for the old man. He found him standing up against the tiled subway wall, next to a bench.

'What's your name?'

The old man recognised him and his anxiety-laden eyes darted left and right.

'I'm just trying to get home. I don't want no trouble.'

'It's OK. It's OK,' he soothed. 'I'm just interested, that's all.' He was the urbane lawyer to an agitated witness.

13

'Ezekiel. Most folk just call me Easy, for short.'

'Well … Easy,' this with a nod of acknowledgement, 'I'd just like to know more about you. The tickertape says we have twenty minutes, so why don't you and I just parley a while to fill in the time?'

'Well, OK,' said Easy, unsure about his own contribution to a discussion with this fine-looking gent with his crisp white collar, fancy rig and cultured tones.

'You see,' ventured Jackson, 'I spend my time at work and play with people who might fancifully consider themselves the cream. Bankers, lawyers, hedge fund managers, politicians, executives. My life is lived in a little triangle between my apartment, my office and my club. I guess the nearest I get to do real life is the bellhop in the apartment block or the receptionist at the health spa. Then I met you today with your little … "predicament".'

Easy pulled a face-shrug.

'… and I thought to myself, well, I suppose, I'd like to know a little bit about you and how you came to be here.'

The old man relaxed a little.

'Ain't so much to tell. Just another bum on food stamps without his train fare, I guess,' said Easy resignedly.

Jackson, with razor-sharp forensic – but unintimidating questioning – teased his story out of him.

Now in his late 60s, Easy was the eleventh of twelve children – all named promisingly and faithfully after biblical characters – born near Alabama. His father had been a farm labourer, his mother in domestic service. He chuckled as he admitted he was no scholar.

'But no stranger to work, sir,' he emphasised.

Crop-picking, livestock, fence-building, pipe-laying, slaughterhouse, Easy had done them all. But mechanisation had driven him off the land into the town. He had held down a factory job near Pittsburgh.

'Never late, never sick, never give them no trouble.'

'So what happened?' queried Jackson.

'Accident. Leastways, that's what they said it was. Got tangled up in the machine. Damn Stop button was disabled and by the time they got me out, so was I. I was good for nothing.'

'So did you sue?'

Easy chuckled again, closed his eyes and said wistfully, 'Old black guys like me don't take on big corporations. I took advice from the Union. Oh! we wrote it up, but they got a big, heavy letter from the company lawyers. Admitted nothing, said there would be big legal costs and they were going to defend it hard. So that was that.'

Jackson nodded his understanding. Menacing letters with vigorous arguments and threats of massive legal fees were standard practice in his world. He called it "positioning the client's negotiating stance" and it was irrespective of the merits of a case. He sometimes wondered what had happened to his youthful earnestness and the Latin watchword of his Professor of Jurisprudence at Yale, which translated as: "Integrity Above All".

Well, as long as he stayed the right side of the line, maybe total integrity was for losers. It was a dog-eat-dog world out there.

'So, how come you're in the City?' asked Jackson with a quizzical frown and a pursing of the lips.

'Well, there's places to live. South Bronx ain't much but you can get a flophouse there. You got food assistance programmes and somewhere to patch you up or get medicine. And I come in when they's running the litter-picking. You know what I mean?'

'Sure,' said Jackson, nodding. 'You're one of those guys with the big bags of coke cans.'

'Yeah, that's it,' agreed Easy. 'You can pick up ten, maybe twenty dollars in a day. Hard on these old black bones but, hey, it's some chow money.'

Jackson warmed to Easy. A lifetime of work – a moment of bad luck. But an indomitable spirit of self-reliance, tempered with the realism of being old and black and not book learnt. He liked the self-deprecating chuckle he gave to underline his story.

Unusually, they quickly struck up an unlikely friendship in the space of ten minutes, with Jackson impressed by the open, honest and humorous character he had got through the turnstile. He was glad he had. He was also glad that he had sought him out to listen to him. Such a diametric contrast to the usual equivocating, deferential, double-crossing, bullshitting, unreliable characters he associated with in business. And that was just his clients. He wondered if there was anything he could do for him. He pulled out his wallet. Damn! No cash. But Easy was already waving him away before anything was proffered.

Jackson wanted to help. He felt the stirring in him of something not motivated by fees or obligations. That wellspring of humanity that gives without thanks, that helps without expectation, that cares but is non-judgmental.

His grandfather had had it with all those schools he had endowed through the trust fund. Somewhere along the line, Jackson had been side-tracked into an exclusively commercial, litigious, avaricious and single-minded world of sharks and fees and balance sheets. That was it – the integrity of the balance sheet but the desolation of the soul.

He saw it now, quite clearly. The seeds of a new and different Jackson Shucksmith had been planted.

'Listen, Easy,' he said in a lawyerly voice that brooked no opposition. 'In a minute I'm going to embarrass the hell out of you, but trust me on this one.'

Easy looked bemused and watched as Jackson hoisted himself up on the bench. The crowd susurrated but paid little attention. He pulled out his Montblanc pen and tapped it insistently on a wall-hung fire extinguisher in the manner of a master of ceremonies. A Doppler hush ran round the crowd of around 200 commuters who turned to look at the tall, impressive dude in the fancy suit.

Was this some kind of transport announcement?

Well, he had no uniform and this guy looked too cool for that.

Maybe a crazy man? Well, he didn't look crazy. In fact, he looked like he'd stepped out of a film.

Jackson looked around the throng, making eye contact with as many as possible on his semi-circular sweep. He was a commanding figure, used to the theatre of public oratory. He waited for total silence and rapt attention.

'We're all strangers here. Thrown together by events. We know the rules on the subway. Get down, get through and get to your stop without tissue damage and keep hold of your money. Oh, and whatever you do, don't engage with your fellow travellers. But the transportation Union has today given us a chance to stop and look around. To look around and see that we're not just fish in a shoal passing through.

'We're all people with needs, and deadlines, and ambitions and families. We've all got our own individual stories. Some will have tragedies, some anxieties. But, just for today and for these twenty minutes, we're part of the Platform 2 downtown family at Columbus Circle. Look around you. That person next to you is worried about their job. That woman has a parent who is ill. That young guy over there worries if he'll make college.

'You're asking yourselves, "What the hell is this fella doing haranguing us? I just want to get on that downtown train."

'Well, my name is Jackson Shucksmith and the reason I'm talking to you is because I want to introduce you to someone I just met. Someone a lot of you walked past the other side of that turnstile. I got him through. Then I just spent ten minutes getting to know Easy here.' He gestured towards the old man. 'And I wanted to tell you that talking to him and listening to his story has changed my life.

'My granddad used to say: "Never forget the little people." Now, I'm a corporate lawyer …' He waited until he got the pantomime hiss, which he acknowledged good-humouredly. '… And I don't meet little people any more. I just help to make big, rich people even bigger and richer. And I'd forgotten that people like Easy here ever existed. They're just not in my line of vision.

'Well let me tell you about him. He's had a tough life and he's had some bad treatment – particularly from some of my colleagues. I'll get on to that. But he's here today. Still standing. Still trying to earn a day's pay. But he came away without even making his subway fare. He wasn't asking for a handout from you. He just wanted to get home. But he isn't angry with you or even his life. He's just one of our family who needs a bit of a lift with his burden today.

'Now, he didn't ask me to say anything. If you look at him …' Jackson turned briefly to smile at Easy, who was looking down whilst embarrassedly shaking his head. '… You'll see that he just wants me to stop speaking and let him slide away home. But he's one of the little guys the family here mustn't forget as we all move around in our own little worlds. Now I know that nobody here has money to burn. But I'm asking you to find it in your heart to help Easy by giving what you can.

'Any accountant here?'

A few people raised their hands. Jackson singled one out.

'You, sir. Yes, you with the hat. Pass that round for me. Now I know some of you will have money troubles of your own. I respect that. But just toss in a quarter. It's a quarter more than Easy's got right now. And if you can toss in five or ten bucks, well, let's show that the family cares. There's a couple of hundred of us here, I guess, so we can make a difference.'

A redneck in work clothes challenged him.

'So what are *you* going to throw in, lawyer?'

This, to accompanying nods and noises from those around him.

'Well,' said Jackson. 'I'm a little like the President. I don't carry money and Easy here doesn't take cards.'

There was a moment of cynical disquiet.

'But I tell you what I *am* going to do. Easy here needs a little legal help with a case to compensate him for injuries he got at work through no fault of his own. Some "colleagues" of mine threatened they'd get hot and dangerous if he looked for redress. Now, when they get a letter from me saying that my company is now representing Easy, I'll give it twenty-four, maybe forty-eight hours before they start talking figures. If *you* want to buy my time, it'll cost you $12,000 a day, plus taxes and expenses. For my friend Easy, here, the bill is zero.'

The crowd made approving whoops and whistles.

'So, Easy. Here's my business card. Here's my hand and here's my heart.'

He grasped the old man's hand. He was shaking his head in disbelief.
Jackson turned back to the crowd.

'Now, where's that accountant guy?'

The man was tallying up the final notes.

'How much you got in that hat?'

'Eight hundred and sixty-one dollars and fifty cents,' he beamed.

'Well, look at that,' said Jackson. 'The family came through.'

The crowd cheered. Jackson stilled them with an upraised hand.

'Today, you have carried on a proud American tradition. Remember the words of Emma Lazarus on that plaque at the base of the Statue of Liberty?

> Give me your tired, your poor
> Your huddled masses yearning to breathe free
> The wretched refuse of your teeming shore
> Send these, the homeless, tempest-tossed to me
> I lift my lamp beside the golden door!

'Well, today you lifted your lamps and shone a light on Easy. And I want to thank you from the bottom of my heart for your good deed. As we all go our different ways, let's never forget the little people, the Easys, and take with us the lesson that, together, we can make a difference.

'I've learned a big lesson today and – trust me, I'm a lawyer.' He waited for the laugh. 'You can be sure I'll be going about my business and my life in a different way from now on. So, Easy, here's the contribution from the family. We hope it makes life just a little sweeter this Thanksgiving.

'But, first thing we've got to do is go and get you a legal ticket. I'll be expecting a call from you tomorrow and we'll get right on to that little matter we spoke about. And if you don't call in, I'll come and find you!'

Jackson stepped out into the winter sunlight down in the financial quarter. He gripped his mobile phone.

'Marjorie, what's the name of that woman from the neighbourhood law centre? You know who I mean.'

'Yes, Mr Shucksmith. Ms Doyle. You told me to busy you up whenever she called.'

'Yes, that's her. I want you to ring her and call her in. We may have something interesting to talk about. Oh, and Marjorie …'

'Yes, Mr Shucksmith?'

'The diary – from next month I want you to block book every Friday. From now on, that will be my day for pro bono cases.'

'Certainly, Mr Shucksmith,' agreed Marjorie, with just a hint of surprise in her voice.

'Now,' said Jackson to himself, 'let's go and do a little shark hunting!'

Going Down Fighting

You never know what you're going to get in A & E.

People are endlessly inventive in ways of incapacitating themselves. They will hurl themselves onto the ground from a selection of vantage points Impale themselves on foreign objects; or on Saturday night, maybe someone else's foreign object. Ingest cocktails of pills and fluids – especially those with little skulls and crossbones you might find under your sink. They will happily concertina cars into walls, headbutt glass patio doors, generously pass on exotic viruses, and variously burn, stab, concuss, poison or exsanguinate and render comatose either themselves or someone else.

As for us, we stitch them, medicate them, pump things in or pump things out, bandage and splint them, dispense advice which will be blithely ignored and mop up their vomit, excretions and blood.

All in a night's work. As Lofty Large says as he walks the field of battle, counting the dead and bayoneting the wounded: 'They're just machines that need repairing.'

You can't let yourself get too involved. In any case, it's difficult to form any emotional attachment to a drunk, tattooed, monosyllabic Neanderthal who's demanding attention for a hand he has just broken on the face of his girlfriend. In my experience the young are demanding, importunate and self-absorbed. Whereas anyone born before ... oh! I guess around 1960 – must have been reading the *Daily Mail* too much! – are stoic, selfless and apologetic about taking up your time, sometimes even as they start to expire before your eyes.

George Aylward was a good example of the type. In his eighties, diminutive and wizened, he was wheeled in late one Friday afternoon, apologising left and right for the trouble he was causing. The paramedics parked him in a bay and we hooked him up. Low blood pressure, pain in the abdomen and lower back, erratic pulse.

'Well, George,' I said in my best medical, matter-of-fact voice, 'what have you been up to?'

'Nothing, nothing,' he winced. 'I was just in the lounge of the hostel watching telly and felt poorly. Eammon on reception called the ambulance even though I told him not to. Sorry, Doc, sorry.'

'Well, you're in the best place, old chap. Let's have a poke around.'

Even a cursory examination showed me George was not a well man. Severe pain in the belly, clammy skin, rapid, fluctuating heartbeat.

'I'm going to have to send you over to our cheery people in scanning. I think I know what's wrong with you, but I want confirmation. Remember to smile nicely for the camera. Though I have to tell you, George, that we're going to have to keep you in and maybe do a few repairs on you.'

'Sorry,' said George, 'for putting you to all this trouble. I've read about us old-timers blocking up the beds.'

'Don't you worry about that. I think you deserve to get something out of the system after all you've put in over the years. Now, is there anyone you want us to call?'

It soon transpired that George was on his own. There had been a wife, Elsie, but his rueful smile told all. A daughter in New Zealand, but he enjoined us not to trouble her right now. She wasn't going to be able to come round and mop his brow.

As I sat with him, filling in charts and notes and taking a medical history, he gave me a potted summary of his modest life. Left school at fourteen, later went into military service, invalided out, tried to make a go of mining but no good. Always in work but his lack of qualifications and his disabilities left him struggling. Elsie helped out, working when she could, but here he was, on a pension and, '… not much good for anything, any more,' he laughed.

I kept an eye on him over the next couple of hours and I began to like old George very much. Despite his pain, he brightened up each time I came to check him and was always ready with a quip.

'Still here, Doc. Hanging on; costing the health service money. You haven't managed to get rid of me, yet; although that nurse had a go.'

Trisha had been a touch brutal looking for a vein for an intravenous saline drip. When she finally succeeded she said, 'There you go, George.'

George said he thought it was a mercy killing.

But George, if my assumptions were correct, was not far off death, anyway; unless we acted fast. I chivvied the CT people and he was eventually wheeled off with a weary thumbs up.

Back forty minutes later, they rang to confirm what I had suspected.

'Triple A. Looks like there's already a leak from a dissection. It's going to blow unless we get him into surgery fast. Dilated to 6.5 centimetres.'

Triple A is medical shorthand for an Abdominal Aortic Aneurysm. Basically, the main artery in the stomach has ballooned. If it ruptures the patient is usually dead within seconds. The problem is particularly common in older males. We had to sort George out fast or he could die in front of our eyes.

When they wheeled him back to A & E I talked him through the findings, pulling no punches.

'So, unless we can do this puncture repair on your inner tube, you're going to deflate quickly and spectacularly, George. Sorry.'

'It's not your fault, Doc. I know you'll do your best for me.'

George looked around the cubicle, more agitated than I had seen him.

'Where's my clothes, my coat?'

'Don't worry, old boy. You're not going anywhere for a while. We'll look after them.'

'No, but there's something I need to check. Something I like to hang onto.'

Trisha located his clothes in a cupboard. He asked for his coat and feverishly searched in an inner pocket. Finding what he was looking for, he subsided onto his trolley, his eyes closed, something grasped in his hand.

'What's that, George? Your lottery ticket? Your lucky rabbit's foot?'

He opened his hand and let me look. It was a rather nondescript medal.

'Just something I got in Korea – 1951. Something they gave me; although there were a lot of other brave men. Most of them aren't with us now. I was lucky. When I picked it up I said it was for the other men in the Gloucesters. Hill 252, it was. You just do what you think is right at the time. Instinct takes over. Anyway, they were all my friends. You couldn't just stand there. You had to have a go.'

I stared for a minute from George, to the medal, and back to George. Something dawned.

'Bloody hell, George. This is a Victoria Cross!'

George shook his head modestly.

'I'm always a bit embarrassed about it. Strange when you get something like this for just doing your job. But keep it to yourself, will you. It always attracts attention and that's not really me. But it'll go with me to my grave, which looks as if it might be sooner rather than later from what you're telling me.'

I told George I would respect the confidence, even though it was something I would be proud to tell others. But now I had to get on to the team to discuss what was the next stage of treatment. I asked if there was anything he needed and told him I would be back soon with an action plan.

Privately, I knew that I would have to have a round table with Hillyer, the cardiothoracic surgeon, and Quarmby, the director of clinical services. Hillyer was practical, unemotional, to the point of being glacial and risk-averse. Quarmby was a bit of a martinet, driven by budgets, throughputs, outcomes and key performance indicators. He saw tricky patients as a bit of a nuisance who could sometimes clog up the effective running of an efficient service. You know the type.

I looked in on George before I went off for my break.

'Not forgotten you, George. Keep smiling. Keep breathing. I'm just having an hour or two's R & R before I come back tonight and talk to people about how we sort you out. I'll be back around 7.00 p.m., so try and get some rest and I'll see you then.'

'OK, Doc. Hope you can fix me up. Not feeling too good. By the way,' he said with a conspiratorial wink, making smoking motions with his hand, 'any chance of nipping outside for a Harry Wragg?'

I smiled and wagged my finger in mock admonition.

Back in my flat after a restorative double espresso, I decided to check out the history of my modest but heroic patient.

Amazing thing, the Internet. Just a few clicks and there it was, the citation for George:

> Private Aylward was part of an advance party of infantrymen of the Gloucester Regiment. His group of thirty men had become inadvertently isolated near the Kimjim River on 12 April 1951 as a result of unexpected enemy insurgency. The two officers attached to the party were wounded and *hors de combat*. The group had retreated to safe ground after coming under heavy fire and being outflanked. Including his commanding officer Captain John Macrae, four infantrymen had been wounded and were stranded on open ground.
>
> Private Aylward, acting in total disregard for his own safety and in full view of the enemy, made incursions into no-man's-land and brought back each of his four wounded colleagues to safety, despite being severely wounded twice himself. Private Aylward acted courageously and selflessly and in the finest traditions of his regiment in bringing his comrades to safe ground where they could be treated. Of the four men, three survived, including his commanding officer, and the party was eventually relieved by covering air fire and

reinforcements. The three survivors each owe their lives to Private Aylward, operating under almost insuperable odds.

I sat back in my chair and thought about this quiet, self-effacing man. Decorated for his courage for thinking about others and now needing a bit of help himself. I nodded to myself.

'Respect, George. It's not every day I come across a real-life hero. I'll do everything I can for you.'

Back at the hospital, I summoned an urgent case conference with Hillyer and Quarmby. We reviewed the case history, the charts, the CT scans, my observations. Hillyer sucked in air through his teeth.

'You will know that we have to measure the risk of surgery against a prognosis without such a radical intervention. Even if he survives the shock of surgery, you know the risk of other associated problems – embolism, stroke, kidney failure, hypovolaemic shock. I could go on. It's not an encouraging picture, given his age and condition.'

Quarmby chimed in:

'And don't forget, we will be tying up valuable and restricted medical resources – theatre, surgeon, ITU, etc. Aftercare could go on for weeks and in any case,' he said, by way of tempering what might be thought to be an overly balance-sheet approach, 'I wouldn't want to put an old man through such a traumatic procedure that is not at all guaranteed to prolong his life.'

So, two resounding "no" votes there and then. I continued to argue the case and finally they relented.

'Well, you can have the final say on this,' said Hillyer, 'as long as you explain to this man all the attendant risks.'

'I will,' I said, 'including the fact that he'll probably bleed to death if we just stand by.'

I went to see George.

'I'll give it to you straight. It's looking pretty bad, George,' I said apologetically. 'We can open you up and do a repair. If it works – and it's a big if – you stand a chance of eventually smoking yourself to death instead. But if we do nothing, the likelihood is that this balloon you've got in your artery is going to pop very soon. In that case, you won't even have time to light up.'

George thought for a while. This was one of those times when a doctor had to shut his mouth and let the patient think things through.

Finally, he looked at me.

'And if I have this surgery, what are the odds of me surviving?'

I thought for a moment.

'Almost insuperable.'

George stopped. Thought. Fixed me with a look. Registered something. Looked at me again and gave me a weak, knowing smile.

'Well, in that case, Doc, we'd better have a go then, hadn't we?'

En Passant

He recognised the tone of the flight announcement even though it was in Mandarin. The rumblings of discontent and gestures of exasperation from the locals confirmed it. The English follow-through in that particular low transatlantic drawl made him screw his face up.

'Unfortunately, we are informed that Beijing Airport is closed owing to recent heavy snowfall. We are diverting to Dalian International Airport. We are sorry for any inconvenience. Passenger safety is our prime consideration.'

He computed the options. This would take a lot of fast footwork. Even though it was Chinese New Year, the client company had organised a local tiger team to turn valves and pull levers. Having your chemical plant losing half a million dollars a day could be very vexing, and Benedict was being parachuted in as hero trouble-shooter.

The ever-smiling and solicitous flight attendant advised him that he would be taken into a hotel in Dalian until the weather lifted.

Immigration and baggage were the usual chaotic shuffle, so he was grateful for the relative quiet of the business-class limo to take him into the city centre. The pace of traffic was funereal. His driver said in halting English:

'Chinese New Year. Everybody move!'

He knew that each year, about this time, around half a billion Chinese made arduous trips home, particularly the migrant workers. They were like salmon returning to their origins and people were swept into an orgy of presents, decorations, feasting and firecrackers.

Driving into the city was like a trip into a war zone, with coruscating showers of sparks and thunderflash detonations. All in an almost literally lunatic attempt to drive away evil spirits and to gain the attentions of the gods of wealth and good fortune.

It was in the genes.

There was certainly much attention-seeking behaviour as they drove into the concrete cliffs of Dalian, one of the new cities that had sprung up after the Great Leap Forward. Benedict knew, from his time in remote chemical plants, that such shiny cosmopolitan centres were in stark contrast to the medieval rural wastes, where subsistence on $2 a day was the usual way of life.

Still, for tonight – maybe for a few nights – he would luxuriate in the cocoon of the business world.

Liveried staff competed to open his car door, retrieve his bag, direct him to the cherry-wood panelled reception. Here was opulence. Granite, marble, voluminous fresh flower arrangements, discreet water features, noiseless escalators to softly lit mezzanines. After the verbal formalities, he was directed to his upgraded presidential suite.

The hotel was eerily quiet after the mayhem in the streets. He surmised that with most businesses shut, hotels for the captains of industry were short of takers. However, this would suit him fine. A shower, a few drinks, some freshly cooked non-airline food and a chance to go through the technical data properly so he would be off and running when he eventually reached the site.

He phoned Pressberger.

'Pete, it's Ben. Beijing is out of action. Snow. We got diverted to Dalian, so I'm in the Emperor Hotel until we get the all-clear. Can you phone Frank Lee and his crew to tell them I'm delayed? They were meeting me off the Emirates, but I don't have their mobiles. I'll email them a project schedule while I'm here and they can start the plan and prep. Don't think I'll be more than a day or two, but I'll keep you posted. New Year here but hotel is dead. Everyone's gone to the moon.'

No one else to call. International trouble-shooting sounded glamorous, but it didn't even leave the time to join a darts club. A year ago, Andrea had given him an ultimatum – me or the job. The choice was made in a nanosecond, but he left it a conscionable time to spare her sensitivities. Better to travel light. Maybe in time, but for now, onwards and upwards.

After a presidential shower, he scanned the world news on the satellite TV whilst appreciatively quaffing the bottle of decent complimentary red. Too seductive to order up room service and then collapse into jet-lagged oblivion. Had to get his biorhythms into local time, so one or two hours over a meal and his laptop would recalibrate his body clock.

There were three restaurants advertised on the wall of the lift:

> Dragon Palace – traditional Chinese cuisine.
> The Raffles Restaurant – 24-hour luxury buffet.
> Café Berlin – an international à la carte dining experience.

Chinese food. Not tonight, he thought. I'll be getting a bellyful of that down on site. Buffet? Too much like hard work. I think the Café Berlin.

He was pleased with his choice. Dark panelling, discreet lighting, smiling staff plus a pleasantly unobtrusive pianist. He slid into a chair on a corner table and opened his laptop, after ordering a fine Sancerre.

No need to hold back, he thought. The client is picking up the tab and this will be just a drop in the ocean if he gets his plant back on stream.

The restaurant was not of the vast, strip-lit canteen variety. Maybe twenty or thirty tables, virtually unoccupied in a crescent shape around a sprung, polished wooden floor. A few quiet drinks, a steak and a little light work. Perfect.

He glanced at his fellow diners. An old couple, taciturn to the point of coma, were finishing their drinks in silence and left without expression.

On another table sat a young woman in a traditional red Chinese brocade dress. Her colouring and stature suggested she was local, but something about her face and Slav cheekbones suggested a more Western background.

She noticed him looking at her and she smiled. He looked away quickly. He knew what this was. Put lone travelling businessmen in an international hotel and all sorts of camp followers congregated. In Moscow or Delhi or Mexico City there would often be a conspiratorial question from the concierge about "company for the evening". In some hotels, you might get a call as soon as you hit your room.

'Hello, my name is Cindy, or Petra, or Jennifer. You sound nice. Can we meet for a drink tonight?'

He had been warned of the pitfalls of foreign travel on the Cultural Acclimatisation Course. Ladies who exhibited an instant liking for you were not actually entranced by your deeply fascinating views on the exchange rate. They had other commercial interests in mind.

Brocade Lady was beautiful, but he knew that eye contact was not advisable. He studied his computer screen and sipped his drink.

'Can I sit with you?'

She was standing by his table.

'Look, I'm busy. I'm just having a quick meal and I need to finish this piece of work.'

'I won't stay long. My name is Xiu Xiu but my English name is Lily.'

His eyes appraised her. Certainly beautiful, she had an open look and raised her eyebrows appealingly. She looked to be an interesting fusion of Chinese and European. If you could rate genuineness through one sweep of eyes, voice and expression, then she certainly qualified.

'I am here on my own. I saw you on your own and I thought we could be company?'

She sat down and looked beseechingly at him. Very hard to knock back such a beautiful waif. As long as he only had a friendly conversation, surely that wouldn't break any rules? As soon as it began to turn into a transaction, the shrift would be very short. Her eyes were vulnerable, her smile childlike.

'I am not used to restaurants, especially in big hotels. I am here for New Year. I live in the country about seven hours on a train, but Dalian is where my grandparents met and where I was born. You know about Chinese New Year?'

Yes, he knew about the annual migration. This approach, if it was an approach, was totally disarming and did not feel like the prelude to a financial discussion about a menu of services.

'I am very contrary. Most people go from the cities back to the country. Me, I go the other way.' This said with a charmingly smothered giggle.

'Your English is very good,' said Benedict.

'I was a translator for a big company; Chinese, English, Russian. I studied hard when I worked in a factory. This was in an office in Dalian. But now I don't work in an office. I am in a factory in Guanghao, a long way away. It is a very hard life.'

'So why are you here?'

'This hotel is the nearest place to where my grandfather and grandmother met many years ago. He was a Russian soldier in Dalian after the war. She was a Chinese girl working in the canteen. This was before all this was built,' she said, sweeping her arm across the twinkling view of the city. 'They were in love but he had to go back to Russia with the army. In those days, no one could marry and settle without Party approval and they did not know the right people.

'When he went back, he didn't know that she was going to give birth to my mother. It was very sad. His name was Vasily. He never did come back, but she told me about him; how they used to dance. Some in my family say that my face is like his. I am, how do you say, like a mongrel.' With another shy, self-deprecating laugh.

'Well, if you are, you're a very attractive one!'

Benedict was bemused. In five short minutes he had heard part of the life history of this beautiful girl and he felt his cynicism melting. The part of his brain which housed the early warning radar was now out of commission for tonight.

'Do you dance?' she asked, with a direct gaze. 'You see, I came back to Dalian to see if I could find someone nice, just to dance with, as my grandmother once did. I love to dance, but in the village where I live now there is no music, no dancing, no nice people. It has cost me two months' wages to buy this dress, travel here and get the smallest meal I can. And when I saw you, I hoped that you would just talk to me and dance with me. I won't stay long.'

He turned over the permutations in his mind. This was either the most oblique come-on he had ever experienced or a softly sad story he had to hear.

Lily's father had been a coal miner, killed while working, as just one among millions of expendable labourers in the primitive mines worked to fuel national growth. Her mother had been run over whilst cycling to work, by a car containing a Party official. It had all been hushed up to save careers.

She had worked in an electronics factory while studying at night, learning and practising English and Russian. She had a well-paid job as a translator but made the mistake of marrying a local man with very patriarchal and violent tendencies.

'He beat me. He drank. There were other women. He was a crazy gambler.'

It turned out that the only way she had to escape the violence and responsibility for his debts was to flee to a remote village, where a friend had found her work. She had taken her daughter, Yuliya, who was now 5 years old.

Benedict listened to this sad tale of a beautiful young woman's life of weary destitution and looked at her searchingly. An almost tangible thaw set in.

'My name is Benedict Madigan,' he said gently. 'That's my Irish name, but my English name is Mad Ben.' He smiled.

She smiled back.

He told her how he had travelled from Ireland to study in England. His father was dead and his mother was in the early stages of dementia. Occasionally, he returned home for Xmas and funerals, but the company was his family now.

She smiled and remarked that he was an orphan and a migrant worker like her.

She said, apologetically, 'Please will you dance with me?'

He led her to the small dance floor and she pressed herself to him as they shuffled in a small circle to the music of the pianist.

With some gentle prompting, she continued her accelerated life history. Her husband had threatened to kill both her and Yuliya. The work she did now was low-level but just enough to pay for one room and feed them. At least she was safe there. But there must be more. The future had looked bright once, but now, in her early thirties, the skies had darkened and it was a struggle to live. So, particularly at this time of year, she felt she must come "home", put on her best dress and try to find somewhere to dance just one more time before rural penury sucked her down into oblivion.

He looked down at her beautiful brown eyes and saw that she was on the verge of tears.

'I don't want a lot out of life. Just an ordinary job, to see my daughter growing strong and intelligent, and just now and then, to dance with someone kind.'

They danced until the pianist, with an apologetic smile, closed the lid of the piano. It seemed natural that they would make their way, wordlessly, to the lift.

Not even his best friends would describe him as a passionate man, so he had no idea where this hungry pulse came from. Stertorous breaths. Tangled bodies. A shudder from his core.

As they lay together, she said, 'I am very sorry. This was a surprise. You must think I am a very bad person.'

'No, Lily, no. This was something that you read about but don't believe.'

She clung onto him.

'You are a kind man, but your dancing is very bad, Mad Ben!'

They laughed together.

They spoke of happenstance. Of serendipity. He must see her again. He wanted to learn more about her. He wanted to meet Yuliya. He came to China regularly. She laughed delightedly.

Reaching for the hotel pen, she scrawled her telephone number on the back of his hand, saying, 'That way you will remember it in the morning. I have to go early to get the train back to the village. I was going to stay in the waiting room. Maybe I can stay here for a few hours?'

She stayed. His body subsided, all of the energy ebbing until he fell into a deep, dead sleep fuelled by travel, wine, jet lag and passion.

The phone jolted him out of his sleep. He was alone.

'Mr Madigan, we have good news. Beijing is now open. The travel company has booked you on the next flight from Dalian. Your car leaves in two hours.'

Pulling back the curtain, he viewed a sparkling blue-and-gold morning which reflected his mood, as he remembered. Life had a new clarity and simplicity today. He smiled and nodded to himself, puffing out his cheeks in a disbelieving smile. As a chemical engineer, he didn't do poetry, but he was reminded of a particular verse that had stayed from long ago in his schooldays:

> And was it a dream, and was there a place
> And is it a hundred years to there,
> Did my lips taste your lips, did my hands cup your face,
> And were there flowers everywhere?

He pulled together his clothes, laptop, jacket. Better check all the documentation.

He looked in his jacket pocket. Where was his wallet? With mounting panic, he searched all the likely places. Nowhere! God! It had everything – tickets, passport, visa, immigration details, sterling, yuan, credit cards – everything!

Then, with an almost piercing pain, it came to him – Lily!

He had been turned over in the stupidest way. He had bought the story. He had been warned but had fallen headlong into the trap. The crash from serenity to anger was precipitate. He cursed himself. He cursed the elaborately wrought story of a consummate con artist. Why settle for a few yuan, when you can clean someone out totally? How many other people had fallen for this before him?

He needed to think about how he extricated himself from this. The company would be mad. The client would be livid. The delays would mean liquidated damages. He had no money for the hotel. He must get on to the consulate. Was there one in Dalian? Hell! all that bureaucracy …

He winced as the implications multiplied.

In the shower, he hit the wall with his fists as he retrieved suitable Anglo-Saxon expletives. He angrily slapped himself in the face. He rubbed off the telephone number on his wrist with raw, primal anger.

Collecting his belongings, he took the lift down to start the long-winded and sobering business of unravelling the mess. Where the hell to start?

At reception, he said, 'Benedict Madigan. I'm afraid I have a problem …'

He was stopped by the smiling receptionist.

'Ah! Mr Madigan. We have something of yours. You must have dropped this in the Café Berlin. Our maintenance cleaners brought it in this morning. It was under a table. Maybe it fell from your jacket.'

Everything was there, untouched. Relief!

Then despair. So it had all been true. It had all been real.

He looked at his wrist.

There was no trace of a number.

Beulah

Well, it's a living. Burying pets was, perhaps, not high on the list of glamorous professions I considered. Lawyer, surgeon, accountant, teacher. These were all jobs you could confidently proclaim over the vol-au-vents and Chardonnay. How did you tell people that you dug holes for distressed owners, in which they could plant their erstwhile companions? So I developed a formula – small family business providing professional services – and left it at that. If they persisted, I told them the unvarnished truth.

'I sell plots of land for people to bury their small, usually furry chums rather than let them leave the back of the vets in a body bag. I run a pet cemetery.'

People were either fascinated or intoned a 'How very interesting', before hastily turning the conversation on to less exotic topics: politics, scandal, sport and soaps. Death, the last taboo, especially when it came to Tiddles and Spot.

Actually, I'm being cynical. People often get more love, devotion and friendship out of their pets than many do from their relatives. Some of the headstones – all part of the service and coming in a variety of stone and lettering – will demonstrate what I mean:

Teddy
Died 21 January 1984, Aged 15
"Faithful Unto Death."

Molly (Arbuthnott) – Tough Little Jack Russell
Died Aged 9
"She Saved Our Lives, We Couldn't Save Hers."

Salsa the Siamese
Left us in December 1993
"See You Again Soon, My Friend."

So, why not? Dad had started it but was now semi-retired. Mum did the books. I did the rest. Front of house. Listen to the story, then steer them delicately on to a range of options. Your basic burial or cremation. A suitable quasi-religious ceremony. Stones on pots to mark the spot. And, of course, aftercare services, if necessary, keeping the grave tidy for a small annual fee. Well, it was a living – maybe not quite the right word.

It was one of those early, blowy spring days in March when Mr Diamond came in. I remember it distinctly because he was in a pinstriped suit and carrying a small, beautifully made mahogany box. A tall, angular man who had clearly seen a bit of action. A broken nose, the odd scar. Huge hands with knuckles like walnuts. A military hair cut. Contrasting with this was his well-made suit. A sober silk tie and well-polished shoes completed the picture.

He'd come to give Beulah, his old fox terrier, a good send-off. I heard a familiar story. She was obedient but sparky. Never held a grudge. Would go all day and had the heart of a lion. Women had come and gone. There were hints of unspecified feckless children, all up to no good. But Beulah had been there in good times and bad times, with her curly tan-and-white wiry body and big, knowing brown eyes, always ready with a canine cuddle. I was taking it all in as a possible script for Mr Disney. There I go again. Mustn't be too cynical. This dog had obviously meant a lot to this tough man, who was visibly upset at this final parting.

He explained that he had wanted to make the box which would be her final resting place.

'Least I could do for her. Gave me some consolation. Used to work in wood.'

He explained that he was going away on urgent business. We did the paperwork. He peeled off some notes from a wad in the inside pocket of his fine suit. Then I left him alone with Beulah in her beautiful polished box whilst he paid his last respects. Was that a moist eye when he shook my hand and asked me to find her a shady spot and take good care of her? A hard man with a soft centre, reluctant to be parted.

For the next seven years a letter dutifully arrived from the solicitors, Sharp & Sharp, with a cheque and a curt little note:

Re annual maintenance fee £75 – cheque enclosed.

And that, as they say, was that. Until one day one August I was doing my early morning rounds, checking the premises and the plots when, to my consternation, I noticed signs of a forced entry. Someone had cut through the perimeter fence.

Worse, some of the headstones had been knocked over and a number of holes dug.

The police came round to make a routine report but weren't much interested.

'Probably the work of cranks, sir. They're not all locked up yet,' said the young constable helpfully.

For the record, they took a list of all the plots affected and the names of the little creatures involved. Strange thing was, only one of the graves was empty – Beulah's. The young policeman clucked knowingly at the unusual name.

'Ha! Reminds me of the Hollywood Robber.' When I asked what he meant he said, 'You might have heard of him in the press a few years back. Used to do armed robberies but always dressed impeccably. One of the old school. They're all in trainers and baseball caps now,' he said regretfully. 'Got him in the end. Just done a long stretch for his last job; although, he got out a few weeks ago. Kept tabs on him for a while just in case, but he seems to be making a go of it. In fact, he seems to have disappeared off our manor now.'

'Why Beulah and what was the job he did he went down for?'

'Armed robbery, sir. That's why I smiled at the name. Beulah the Jeweller. A business up in Ashby. But they got him via an identity parade. Never did find the stash, though.

'Now – what's the name of Beulah's owner?'

Faites Vos Jeux!

Wragby must have been born in the Year of the Rat. His shifty, small dark eyes set in a thin, pointy face were always scanning the vicinity for threats or opportunities. The similarity was accentuated by an occasional twitching of the mouth and nose in an otherwise expressionless face. A small brown body shuffled around on noiseless feet. As well as the look of him, his behaviour matched that of an opportunistic rodent. When some drunken hail-fellow was dispensing unwise largesse down at the Catford Arms, Wragby would appear – just as quickly as he disappeared when there was a whip-round for some local unfortunate.

And he shared that rat-like instinct for survival. Without paid employment since the early end of a totally undistinguished and pointless schooling, Wragby somehow got by. He made a turn on a second-hand car after becoming proficient at winding back odometers. He occasionally "collected" for South London loan sharks, with no mercy shown to single mothers who had overreached themselves at Xmas. He supplemented his expert exploitation of the benefits system by liberating electrical goods, computers and radios from negligently parked lorries and cars. Hand-to-mouth; bob-and-weave; low profile; sink or swim epitomised his twilight existence.

But Wragby's overriding passion was gambling. The flashing, coloured lights and symbols of a one-armed bandit would fascinate him. And he had developed a sixth sense for the sequence of configurations which preceded a worthwhile winning tumble of coins. He dabbled in online poker, careful to steer clear and drop out of any game that looked as if anyone competent was playing. There were always enough starry-eyed mugs to provide a steady, if irregular, income.

But his main haunt was the betting shop. Despite crippling innumeracy for the banalities of life such as bills, budgeting and loan rates, he could explain – without missing a beat – why 13–8 was a better return than 6–4 and how to compute quickly the value of a winning Yankee, accumulator or placepot. He fancied himself as a student of form, taking into account variables such as course, distance, jockey, weights, going, trainer, as well as the more arcane pointers that the average punter would not be party to; such as how far the horse had travelled, whether or not the stable was in form, the lineage of the horse and the like.

Most people who bet will tell you that they "just about broke even on the day", which means they have lost. Wragby generally made a turn. Although never spectacular, the experience was rewarding enough to keep him in play. He was like a trained rat, conditioned to press a pedal for a reward and which will keep on pressing it even when the rewards start to become variable. Wragby made just enough to keep him coming back. He was not "addicted" in the sense that some pleasure centre in the brain screamed to be satisfied, but enough neural circuits would light up and just enough winning slips were cashed in to keep him an active player.

His long-suffering partner was Bridie. You could see from her face that at one time she had been beautiful, but now she looked older and more careworn. She hated Wragby's dismissive attitude, his secretiveness and the uncertainty about when or whether he would be appearing again in the dismal, two-bedroomed tenement flat she occupied with two small, etiolated Wragby offspring.

What had once seemed like a carefree and freewheeling existence had long since resolved into a threadbare, week-to-week struggle. Those outside this world with steady incomes, savings, a car to drop the children off at swimming or riding, a house with a garden, could never understand the grinding cheerlessness of her bleak life. Other women might obsess about their wardrobe or the next pedicure – Bridie worried about security, her future and the seeming futility of it all. Unexpected bills, shopping in the supermarket's remaindered goods section and worry about the children were part of her mundane existence.

And, amongst this, Wragby was little help; just another complicating factor. She had to organise, clothe, feed and raise the children. It was she who dealt with threatening paperwork and eked out a subsistence budget with sporadic payments from Wragby. And it was Bridie who attempted to organise their collective legal and financial domestic formalities when necessary, with little or no input from the transient head of household.

For the time being, she thought, there was little alternative. But the germ of a plan had started to spring up in her daydreams. One day soon, she would be free of his comings and goings, his apathy, the squalor of their existence. But it would take some organising. Occasionally she smiled a secret smile and, when she was sure Wragby was well away, she would take out the tin from behind the bathroom panelling. She had privately amassed over £2,000 – part of her eventual passport to freedom and the sunlit uplands. The money was made up of small gifts from her parents, the scrimpings from numerous part-time jobs, and whatever savings she could secrete from the strained household inputs and outputs.

One day she would be free. She had a dream of going back to Ireland to live near her parents. Maybe renting a small house, getting a steady job, seeing the kids flourish at last; perhaps even meeting someone who would treat her decently and maybe even love her.

Wragby, meantime, now simply viewed Bridie as the unpaid but necessary organiser of his needs. Doing the washing, cooking and ironing, looking after the brats, doing the things that women should do, and sorting out the tedious bureaucracy of life, while he focused on his little earners. He saw Bridie as his factotum, occasionally troublesome but worth persevering with as, currently, the benefits outweighed the disadvantages.

One hot, late July afternoon Wragby was to be found in Bennions, the bookmakers, selecting his afternoon portfolio of bets. He noticed a smartly suited male punter of middle age studying the *Racing Post* next to him. The man was flipping the pages back and forth between two race meetings at Fontwell and Wetherby, whilst circling odds, writing small calculations and making low, personal noises of approval. The man looked well turned out and prosperous – not the normal class of haunted derelict expected to be passing the afternoon in a place like this. Wragby was intrigued.

'Any luck?' ventured Wragby.

'Not a question of luck,' said the suit. 'I'm an investor, not a punter. Gambling is a mug's game. Ever seen an unhappy bookie?'

Wragby agreed that he had not. Unused to social small talk, he was nevertheless desperate to find out how this man could be selecting his bet so confidently. He had already noticed him collecting his winnings twice.

'So how do you do it, then? Got a system?' enquired Wragby, keen to find a way of upping his ratio.

'I guess you might call it that,' replied the stranger, a mite dismissively. 'But it's not rocket science. The bookies provide you with all the science you need, free of charge. Look,' he said, now turning to Wragby and humouring him. 'I'll let you into a little secret. Why do the bookies make a horse the favourite?'

'Well,' hesitated Wragby, 'it's because it has the best chance of winning.'

'Correct,' said the stranger, 'but in order to cover themselves, the stronger the chance of winning the ...' He made a rolling gesture with his fingers.

'The shorter the odds!' replied Wragby exultantly.

'You're getting there,' he smiled. 'But even with short odds, can you tell me, approximately, what are the chances of a favourite winning?'

'No idea,' said Wragby. 'I tend to look for value based on a combination of all those things that the ordinary punter overlooks.'

'Well, you might be lucky from time to time and get, say, a 35–1 shot coming up because of some freak factor that no one else has spotted. But it's 35–1 for a reason and will only pay out so infrequently that you're wasting your stake. No, I ran the results from every race meeting in the UK for a complete year; and I can tell you that, apart from random fluctuations, a favourite will get home in one out of every three races.

'Look at yesterday's results if you don't believe me. Now, more punters with only a passing grasp of mathematics' – Wragby silently accepted that the description accurately fitted himself – 'will do mad things like betting on favourites but then, when one doesn't make it, they …' Again inviting Wragby to complete his analysis.

'They double up.'

'Precisely,' said the man, 'and that way madness lies. If you try to fold a piece of paper in half again and again, after about thirty-two folds – if it was possible – it would be thick enough to reach the moon. It's the same with the doubling-up principle. Bet like that on a day when there's a bad run of outsiders and you'll be bankrupt before the afternoon is out.'

'So,' hesitated Wragby, trying to grasp the concept, 'how do you avoid that and still make money?'

'Easy,' said the man. 'You start with a simple and limited aim of trying to make one unit of profit. Your unit might be £1 or £10 or £1,000 – whatever.'

'I still don't quite get it,' frowned Wragby.

'Well, imagine all the favourites on a particular card are 2–1 and you wanted to win a unit of £10.'

'So,' hesitated Wragby, 'I would put a fiver on and if it got home, I'd have my £10 unit.'

'Precisely,' he said. 'But what if it has an off day and doesn't justify its favouritism?'

'Well … I've lost my fiver and I still want to earn my unit of £10. So … the next bet at odds of 2–1 will be £7.50!'

'Correct,' said the stranger. 'It gets home at 2–1 and you win £15. You've won your tenner. You've recouped the fiver you lost from the first race and, of course, you get your stake of £7.50 back. Result – happiness! And so on for the next race. At a ratio of one favourite winning in every three races, you soon make your units.'

'That's brilliant,' said Wragby. 'Why isn't everyone doing it?'

'Well, partly because they're stupid and follow form not mathematics, and partly because if you do have an adverse run, you can be betting quite sizeable amounts just to get a relatively small unit of profit. Most punters don't carry that amount of spare cash around. And what's more, the bookies will soon rumble you if it starts to become obvious what you are doing.'

'Yeah,' said Wragby thoughtfully. 'How do you manage that?'

'Well,' said the man. 'I run two race cards simultaneously: one in the bookmakers and one on a phone account. If I switch from one to the other, the winnings and stakes are randomised and they'll be none the wiser.

'For example, today I'm following Fontwell and Wetherby. Conveniently, they alternate at fifteen-minute intervals. I'm using cash here and a telephone account with Corcorans. I irregularly change both the betting shop and the telephone account so I stay ahead of their security boys. And I'm not greedy. I aim to make about £1,000 a week and that's from different bookies. So I'm well below the radar.'

'Brilliant!' said Wragby. 'I'm going to have a crack at this. Haven't got a mobile phone, but I can get a bit of cash together and there's four bookies in town. Cheers, mister! You've made my day!'

Wragby went outside for thinking time over a cigarette. He checked the previous day's papers. The guy was right! The results at Wolverhampton and Kempton showed twelve races, of which favourites actually won five! An even better strike rate! He computed the unit that he would like to win each week – about £500 would be tidy – and, with some difficulty, worked that back to £100 a day over twelve races at two different tracks, with three favourites winning.

He had found the Holy Grail, the secret of turning base metal into gold. Now he just needed to get his covering stake together and it was next stop El Dorado!

His face fell. He would need cover of around three to four grand to see out a particularly bad run of losing favourites, and that was not the sort of money he could readily put his hands on. Then he had a narrow-eyed, thin-lipped brainwave. The tin behind the bathroom panelling! He had raided it before for smallish sums but had not risked the wrath of Bridie by making serious depredations.

But this was – as the man said – an investment. He could use the cash, turn it into a significant profit and get the money back into the tin before she even noticed. He also considered he might need a supplementary float and Bigboy Bell, the loan shark he worked for, would probably advance him another grand or two.

He treated himself to a couple of celebratory pints of Guinness, all the while marvelling at the simplicity of the scheme and wondering what he would do with his weekly windfall. He agreed with himself that this would enable him finally to break free of Bridie. And those kids were always crying and bawling. Like the self-centred rodent he was, he felt no compunction about taking what he needed and then getting to somewhere warmer and more personally congenial.

He made his way back to the flat via his usual rat run. Bridie was waiting with her customary catalogue of complaints and demands – a gauntlet he knew he had to run to effect his necessary pit stop.

'It would be good if you would tell me sometime when you're coming home.'

'I had to take the little one down to the doctors yesterday. A little help would have been appreciated.'

'You'd better sign this council tax mandate or we'll have the bailiffs round.'

'How can I plan any food if I never know where you are?'

He fended off the brickbats and complaints, signed the mandate quickly, then scuttled into the bedroom and closed the door. She really didn't need to go on like that, he thought. After all, I provide for her and the kids; and I don't beat her.

Satisfied with this personal exoneration, he stayed just long enough to extract the cash surreptitiously from the tin in the bathroom. She wouldn't notice it gone and he would be able to replace it in a couple of weeks. He was just using it temporarily to invest.

He sidled out of the dreary flat. Bridie, saddened by the way her life had deteriorated, busied herself with the children. And she didn't like to create a scene in front of them. No point in having a knock-down, drag-out fight with him. She knew it was a finite problem. She knew where she was going. And she knew how to get there.

Having spent the night on his friend Beggsy's sofa, and secured the loan from Bigboy ('I want it back by next weekend, by the way. You know the rules.'), he staked out his targets. To be doubly safe, he would oscillate between three close-set bookmakers. He bought the newspapers and selected meetings at Lingfield and Haydock. Nice, small fields; clear favourites but not odds-on, which would complicate matters and unnecessarily up the ante. Start times at helpful fifteen-minute intervals.

Bridie dropped the children off at the childminder's and arranged for her friend Stephanie to have them for the evening. She had attempted to retrieve her savings from the secret cache but noted, with a suitable expletive linked to Wragby's name, that the chancer had taken it. Never mind. She made her way to the building society (Instant Loans! Approval in fifteen minutes!) and presented the joint application, helpfully signed the previous evening by a retreating Wragby.

Of course, there was an element of fiction in there, but who was to know? Anyway, they were falling over themselves to lend money at those rates of interest.

After a short meeting with an undermanager who had just graduated from in-Company Smile School, she asked for the whole £10,000 in cash – large notes. She explained that the builder and his subcontractors all preferred the green folding stuff. She stowed the money in an inaccessible zipped pocket in her shoulder bag.

Wragby's first race was at 14.00 hours. A maiden fillies' six-furlong sprint at Lingfield. The favourite, at evens, was Trip the Light, but it struggled in fourth of eight. Not to worry, he thought. The system – no, correct that – the mathematics meant it was just a matter of time before the daily unit was pocketed. Scuttling greasily between bookies, he was only mildly put out when the next three favourites suffered a similar fate. Still, it only required a couple of favourites out of twelve to come home and that was job done for the day.

Bridie put on her only posh frock and an astrakhan overcoat that her parents had bought her for her thirtieth birthday some time previously. With her hair up, make-up carefully applied and a faux diamond brooch sparkling in her lapel, she thought she looked as near the part as she could be. Through some basic research, she had identified the Wessex Club as her prospective venue. Open from early afternoon, it offered no-limits poker, blackjack and roulette.

She knew this was a wild aberration, but desperate women take desperate measures. She had been struck by a news item some weeks previously. A young man with debts and a big mortgage had risked all the money he could gather together on one trip to a casino in Las Vegas. One spin and he had doubled his money. Problems all solved. If this worked, she was free of Wragby and home to Ireland with a deposit for a little house. If it failed, well, there would be a serious reckoning and the problem of how to pay off a loan of that size. If so, she would just have to take a couple of jobs. In any case, Wragby would have half the problem.

At that moment, Wragby had problems of his own. Favourites five, six and seven had all failed to oblige. The stake to win back his losses and make his paltry £100 unit was now into several hundred pounds. But he knew that a favourite would come up eventually. He just had to keep his nerve. But he was now starting to attract somewhat anxious glances from the betting shop assistants as the stakes mounted.

Bridie found the Wessex Club down what was almost an alley off Regent Street. A doorman in evening dress welcomed her in, and smiling attendants took her coat and led her through to a dimly lit casino. There was a dull hubbub of activity. She cashed in all of the £10,000 for a series of multi-coloured chips. The cashier smiled but seemed to think it was quite normal behaviour. Weird how all that money was so quickly and easily translated into some colourful children's counters. She still could not quite believe that she, a quiet Irish girl with a strict Catholic upbringing in a country backwater was really here doing this.

She had decided – because of the story of the young man – on roulette. She thought that choosing a particular number was the quick road to ruin, so she watched the other players for a while. A Middle Eastern-looking man was covering a series of squares in four quarters in what looked like fairly random fashion. But he was winning the occasional small sum. A fat business type – one of a post-lunch party who were egging him on – was choosing random numbers at long odds based, it seemed, on children's birthday dates. He tried little stacks of chips and there was loud cheering when a number came up. But his small wins were very intermittent. She noted that there was an evens chance in red or black. That was the way to go.

Wragby was now in some shock. He had picked the very two damn race cards where favourites were all conspiring to thwart his scheme. After drawing another blank on race numbers eight, nine and ten, he sat down to take stock, looking wildly left and right. He stayed with the formula for race eleven. Another blank! The last race of the twelve was at Haydock where the favourite, at odds of 6–4, was unhelpfully titled Oh Dear Oh Dear. He was not encouraged.

He checked the other courses. At Newbury – he wished he had chosen Newbury – two favourites were already home and hosed after only five races. In the last race there was a small field of four. The favourite was called Happy Returns. He laboriously totted up his losses and counted his remaining stake money.

Bridie was getting the hang of it from watching the other participants. She was also noting the sequence of black/red returns. She mentally placed a bet after a particular run of one colour: three blacks. Next one must be red; try £1,000. Yes! She was winning, if only notionally.

'*Faites vos jeux?*' asked the croupier.

Bridie looked at him quizzically.

'Place your bets,' he translated helpfully.

'Oh, yes. In a minute,' she said, her heart beginning to pound as she neared the abyss.

She told herself to wait for another short run of one colour. She knew it was always a fifty-fifty chance, even if there had been ten blacks in a row. But somehow, she thought, it enhanced her chances. Finally, with a puff of the cheeks and an exhalation of breath after a run of four blacks, she put all her chips on red and watched the croupier spin.

Wragby was feeling like a cornered rat: bookies, horses, that damned stranger with the brilliant idea. They were all against him. Here he was, simply trying to win his modest daily unit of £100, and by the eleventh race his cumulative lost stakes were nearly £2,000. He could feel himself sweating. Bigboy was not going to be happy.

He checked his remaining cash: just a little under £2,000. Pull out now? Stick with the script and go for the final short price nag at Haydock? Surely this one would get home. Or go for the Newbury horse on a course which seemed to be returning favourites? Gritting his teeth, he decided to double up and throw everything onto Happy Returns at Newbury. The name was a sign, he was sure.

At the casino, the croupier gave Bridie a gracious, sideways acknowledging nod as he pushed another £10,000 worth of chips towards her returned stake. The Middle Eastern man pulled a rueful face while the fat businessman said:

'Well done, love. Fearless betting, that. Give it up now while you're well ahead.'

Bridie thought she might consolidate at that. But then she reminded herself that £10k of that money was earmarked for the building society. If she could just pull that off again, then she really would be looking at a golden escape route. She toyed with the idea of just risking half. But then – now watched by a small gathering crowd – she suddenly thought to hell with it. Let's double it!

She staked everything on red again. The croupier acknowledged her brave gamble. The white ball spun round the roulette wheel again and settled into a slot.

'Sixteen red,' said the croupier.

Some applause and a few whistles broke out. Bridie stacked the £40k worth of chips in front of her neatly and watched the next couple of spins. Both black. An invisible hand was pulling her to the cash desk. But a devil inside her head said, 'That was so easy. Imagine if you pulled it off again. How good would that feel?'

She shoved the teetering stack of chips onto red. It had favoured her before. Surely it wouldn't let her down one last time? And when it came up she would have cleared the impossible fortune of £70,000!

The croupier, in his normal fashion, sent the ball the opposite way to the revolution of the wheel and it clattered up and down.

* * *

Wragby had made his mind up. He had to go for it. Everything doubled up on Happy Returns at Newbury. Bet placed. Meanwhile, he listened to the commentary of the earlier race at Haydock and couldn't believe what he was hearing. Oh Dear Oh Dear almost walked in – a winner by ten lengths at odds of 2–1 favourite. He cussed the horse, the jockey, the bookies, the world, himself. He screwed up the newspaper. Well, it was all or nothing now.

The hypnotic voice announced that they were off at Newbury. Happy Returns was an easy-paced, early leader and Wragby rode with him as the commentator said the jockey looked relaxed, had a double handful and was in control. Wragby unfroze a little.

With two furlongs to go, the commentator suggested there might be a challenge from Daring Damsel, but probably too far back to trouble the leader. Inside the final furlong the voice became more agitated. Daring Damsel was putting in a late run and Happy Returns was beginning to tire after leading the entire race.

As they crossed the line, the voice, almost falsetto with excitement now, said: 'And it's a photo!'

In the casino, as the ball was ready to be launched, the croupier called:
'*Faites vos jeux.*'
Bridie suddenly and inexplicably transferred all of her chips from red onto black! Why, she didn't know. She clamped her hand over her mouth and the table, understanding the magnitude of her decision, fell silent. All attention turned to the tumbling white ball.
'Black twenty-two.'
A security man with a walkie-talkie came over to see what the noise was about. The croupier made reassuring noises and he nodded assent and backed off.

Bridie leaned back against the back of the high chair and closed her eyes for a while as she felt the tension drain out of her. That was definitely, certainly, unequivocally and finally the last bet she would ever make in her life. She could take no more. She thanked the croupier and on advice from the Middle Eastern man, pushed him over a £100 chip. Then she took her haul, unbelieving and wide-eyed, to the cash desk.

Wragby wouldn't be back till late and by that time, she and the kids would have packed a few bags and taken a taxi – as they say about big winners – to a hotel at an undisclosed address en route to a new life. And all because the little voice had told her to double up!

* * *

Wragby sat desolate. A nose, he thought. The stupid length of a stupid horse's stupid nose. His wedge had disappeared. There was a loan to reimburse to Bigboy, and Bridie would be like a hurricane when her money was not returned. In his pocket was just loose change. He thought about his mistake and said softly to himself, reminded of the stranger's words:

'Doubling up, eh? That way madness lies.'

Bridie, smiling quietly to herself on the Tube home and hugging her bag, had a very different view.

A Gift from God

As the plane throttled back and began to head east, he pulled out the bulky Manila envelope. Opening it, he found a schedule of all the information that the client had briefed him on. Photocopies of some old press clippings. An artist's reconstruction of what the boy might look like now. A description of the distinctive birthmark on his left shoulder. A large amount – it made him whistle softly – of local currency for ... "as necessary". Money for payoffs. Name, position, reason and amount required. And a copy of the contract. An initial payment of £25,000 (it was already banked – he had checked) plus all necessary expenses (to be fully itemised and receipted, the contract said) and – he still couldn't quite believe it – a payment of a quarter of a million pounds for success. "Success" was simply defined as incontrovertible identification and location of the boy.

He reeled the spool back to the first meeting in the country house drawing room.

A flunky had shown him in – rich people liked to keep you waiting and make an entrance; it was a power thing. The house, the room, reeked of money. Always the same with the nouveau riche. They used their new wealth to buy old things. Houses, pictures, porcelain, clocks. Still, this was classy – he couldn't deny it; although a little antiseptic! That was how 'the client', Mr Bentley and his wife, had come across. He had moved a small occasional table to write down some of the story. When he got up to shake hands on the deal and go, both of them moved in to return it, surreptitiously, back to where the original indentations of the legs had been.

No, he had not warmed to them. Mr Bentley, he knew from the press, had been an ex-boxer who had used his prowess to invest in property. Fortuitous, fortunate, clever, oppressive – who knows? He had made his pile. His wealth had bought him a place where he could be comfortable amongst similarly rich business people and minor aristocracy. A minor gong for services – big donations – to his political party and a life of country house parties, polo,

Henley, Cowes, the Royal Enclosure, confident in the purchasing power of his reputation and his bank balance. Money gave him that pseudo-patrician air. It gave her a three-string pearl necklace and a couple of rocks on her fingers that you would have to remove quickly if she fell in the swimming pool.

Still, Dooley wouldn't wish it on anybody, losing an only son. He had thought of his own son – a useless waster. Failed exams, a series of menial jobs and never-to-be-realised rock band ambitions. But he was still his son. So he had identified with Mr Bentley's story.

'It has blighted our lives, Mr Dooley. Can you imagine one minute being a family on holiday with their 18-month-old boy and the next thing, nothing?'

He couldn't. He already knew some of the story, revived by the press for a good, silly season column-filler from time to time.

They had been on holiday on a Greek island. The boy, Patrick, had simply disappeared from the beach, apparently off the face of the earth. The hullabaloo. The search. The press campaign. The rewards offered. Apparent sightings which had come to nothing. Nearly twenty years on, still looking, still hoping.

Chances were, he mused, that the boy had been abducted by a local nutter. Or maybe swept out to sea, a victim of tide and wind.

There had been no other children. The campaign had become their child, lavishing attention and money and in return getting only frustration, disappointment and heartache. Sounded familiar.

He had asked them why they had chosen him, particularly. There were plenty of other private detectives. He had been recommended, by chance, by Lady Harrington. He remembered her all right. Bored and dissatisfied with her cloistered life, she had done what many previous aristos before her had done. Only she had done it everywhere and omnivorously. With stable grooms, tennis coaches, farmers' boys, the local publican. She had a penchant for the outdoors, so the photographic proof had been easy.

But she had clearly outflanked him. Spotted his car – very unprofessional, that – tracked him down and arranged a meeting in a London hotel. He had liked her. She was pretty, sparky and prepared to offer him more money than her spineless husband. There was even a hint … more than a hint … of services upstairs in the hotel to clinch the deal. That had been very unprofessional, but memorable. He didn't think that real ladies did that sort of thing.

This was her final favour. A thank you for so comprehensively and finally putting his chinless lordship right off the scent.

So here he was, £25K richer already, an all-expenses-paid holiday across any of the Greek islands he might choose and just a chance – but zero on the roulette wheel – that he might turn something up.

More like a needle in a haystack. The zero was 35–1. Leafing through the comprehensive guidebook he had bought, he read that there were more than 2,000 islands belonging to Greece, of which more than 100 were inhabited. Numbers were approximate, it said. So where to start?

There were several main groups of islands. The Ionian to the west of Greece, with Corfu and Cephalonia amongst them. But to the east there was a veritable confusion. The Cyclades, the Sporades, the Northern Aegean, Argo-Saronic (never seen those advertised in the travel agents), the Eastern Aegean and the Dodecanese. Worse still, to get round at all you had to rely on a flotilla of ferries, boats, catamarans and hydrofoils run, he suspected, with the usual pathological Greek approach to timetabling.

The boy had been lost on Rhodes down in the Dodecanese. But there was no guarantee he was there or even in Greece at all, he mused, eighteen years on, with 2,000 islands. What were the odds – a billion to one? Still, he liked a punt, and a free holiday in the sun with a sizeable wedge already banked was not unwelcome.

The baggage handlers were on strike at Athens Airport and the taxi driver who drove him to the hotel was clearly in the early stages of some mental illness – brought on, considered Dooley, by driving an old banger without air con in the mayhem that passed for traffic control in Athens.

He rang his old sparring partner Stelios, to call in a favour he owed him from his old days coppering in South London. Stelios had had enough of the drugs scene.

'It's all Chinese, Jamaicans and Russians now, Dooley. Don't know the rules. Can't make a decent living any more.'

So he had retired back to his roots.

As the car snaked up the hillside to chez Stelios, Dooley thought that Stelios had made a wise choice. Pink-washed, split-level and with a pool overlooking an exquisite vista of colour and sea, the villa blended beautifully into the surrounding countryside as Stelios had blended back into his Greek life. Although after a glass or two, it was apparent that he had not fully embraced retirement and, as Dooley had suspected, had an encyclopaedic knowledge of the Greek demi-monde. Of course, he had heard about the case of Patrick Bentley.

'For me, it's very sad. If the Greeks are good at one thing, it is family.'

But as for any specifics, he could not help. However, tapping the side of his nose, he suggested that Ioannis in Thessalonica would know something, if anybody did.

'He's nice man. Brings in pretty ladies from Albania, the Philippines, Thailand, anywhere. Good money for ladies. Makes tourists happy, eh? Body shop,' chuckled Stelios with an accompanying gesture and knowing pull of the face that signalled a secret understanding amongst the male fraternity.

And with a final bear hug of an embrace and the name of a super pimp in Thessalonica, Stelios had repaid his favour.

Ioannis operated out of an office at the back of a legitimate dry-cleaning business downtown. A fat man with fingers the size of Montecristo No. 2s and the inevitable Greek colonial moustache. He was friendly and earnest but protested that this was not his field.

'Many, many ladies. Good, clean, black, brown, big, small …' He was a veritable shopping catalogue. 'But not boys. We do not have the boys. We never have the boys. My business is good, happy business. Make everybody happy. Make everybody money.'

Clearly, Ioannis' social services department did not extend to those with somewhat more off-the-wall tastes and Dooley was not even sure that he was still on the right track. But Ioannis was happy to try to help a friend of Stelios. His fat, smiling face blackened for an instant and he advised Dooley to search out Philippos with the kind of look you would reserve for a cockroach you had chanced upon in your *salade niçoise*.

And so it was after several more days of hanging around airports and interminable ferries that he found himself on the island of Skiathos. The name of Philippos was clearly well known and disliked even in the seedier haunts of Skiathos town. The mere mention of his name brought a variety of repressive shrugs, frowns and gestures of distaste, but none were prepared to admit knowing him until one wizened old barfly, tempted by a fat, folded bunch of notes, had given a mobile number.

Philippos was a thin, nervy man with a haunted air. Even in the deserted, tiny dark basement bar in which they met he kept looking round as an animal would for signs of threat. Dooley had to pass a series of subtle tests to demonstrate that he was not from the authorities. A brown envelope was tendered. Philippos looked nervously around, quickly thumbed the contents with a practised air and hastily stashed it in an inside pocket. Yes, he remembered the case of Patrick Bentley.

'He was not one of mine but I know. We know. Maybe he is still there. I cannot say. Maybe dead. Who knows?'

Dooley was to find a small Greek restaurant on Alonissos called Dionysos.

'The owner is Costas. But you must be careful and you must not speak of Philippos. Anyway, so many years. Who can be sure?'

And with that, after a final twitchy check around, he was gone.

Dooley emailed an interim progress report back to the Bentleys, saying he had nothing definite but that some interesting leads had narrowed his search down to one outside possibility and that he hoped to be in touch soon. For an outlay already approaching fifty grand, it was not an exciting return. Still, the bloke was loaded and – although he always tried to keep his feelings out of it – it was his only son and heir.

Alonissos was quiet. Apparently, it was a nature reserve and as yet untouched by the great unwashed looking to get lagered or laid, usually both.

The Dionysos was easy to find. Dooley had holed up in a small family hotel in Alonissos town and the dapper concierge had directed him to it.

He had taken a trip up there one afternoon. The hire car spluttered asthmatically along the coast and up the track to the small village – village was perhaps an over-ambitious word – on a rocky outcrop overlooking a picture postcard bay. The restaurant, in truth,was a bar with a few desultory locals gratefully knocking back their shots of ouzo and retsina bought with state handout euros.

Dooley had to admit, though, that the place had potential. A square terrace with, perhaps, a dozen tables overlooked an almost sheer drop to the cobalt Aegean. Sinking a coffee and a Marlboro Light, even he appreciated the late afternoon sun on an orderly jumble of amphorae and terracotta pots with their cascades of asphodels and scarlet geraniums. The terrace was shaded by a trellis of vines and the breeze coming up the rock face from the sea brought a living hum of summer insects mingling with the scent of lavender.

He ordered a meal, lingering over the coffee as his practised eye appraised the personalities who came and went. Mine host Costas was a large man who had clearly spent some years overindulging in red wine, olive oil and cheese. A big, cheerful man, he looked after the bar, swapping important political comment with the locals but instantly snapping into attentive broken English when Dooley ordered. Costas relayed instructions in Greek through a small hatch, when Dooley glimpsed a harassed old woman in black surrounded by tomatoes, olives, fish, cheese and bread, dutifully preparing the various orders.

The food was brought out by a younger, plain carbon copy of the old woman. She quickly and shyly, almost unobtrusively, served the food and drink, cleaned up and added a new bill for customers' beer, wine and coffee to shot glasses on each table. But apart from these three and the customers, there was no other likely individual to attract his attention.

He got into conversation with Costas as the evening began to sink on the bay. He told him he was there on holiday for some peace and quiet after an acrimonious divorce and a hard year in business. He was just touring around with nowhere particular to go, but he liked the peace of Alonissos and complimented Costas on his beautiful restaurant. Costas beamed:

'Business is very hard. But we are just a family and we do not need much money.' He bemoaned the lack of ambition amongst the local politicos on Alonissos. 'We need hotels, roads, water parks. Many British and Germans then come to Costas for Greek food and music. Plenty money. I must pay for my boy at university.'

Dooley's antennae tuned in.

'You have a son?'

'Yes. Theo. Good boy. Very intelligent. He is becoming civil engineer and he makes me very proud, bringing water to the islands.'

Further subtle questioning established that in a few days, Theo would be coming home for vacation.

Over the next few days Dooley was a regular and began to ingratiate himself with the family. The shy daughter smiled when he came in, acknowledging him. Costas dragged his tiny wife from the kitchen and introduced her. She was all acquiescence and deference, wiping her hands on her apron.

Some days he stayed there most of the afternoon and evening, making small talk and establishing himself if not as one of the family, at least as a welcome and trusted fixture on the corner table of the terrace.

He began to like Costas. His wild ambitions for the restaurant were incompatible with his nature. He was generous with his time and his bottle of ouzo. Occasionally he would climb on a small, old, petrol-driven scooter and take the road down to the port to pick up necessaries. Once, the bar ran out of Marlboro Lights, but he kicked the complaining old motor into life and emerged triumphant and beaming an hour later with Dooley's smokes. Costas invited him to dinner.

'Just family, but you can come, my friend. We celebrate Theo coming home. He has a girlfriend, Angeliki. Very pretty. She is going to be a doctor. Very good family. On Sunday night the restaurant will be closed except for you, my friend.'

On Sunday night, Dooley presented himself with some gifts for the family. A silver crucifix for the daughter; he had noted her almost medieval obeisance to religion. A fine lace tablecloth for Mrs Costas and a fine watercolour of the bay, with the restaurant a green, red and blue jewel visible at the top of the picture for Costas. They were effusively grateful. Much wine was poured as a trickle of relations appeared. The sun began to go down and Dooley found himself tapping to the music as he swapped pleasantries at the long oblong table, rearranged for the occasion.

Was it balalaika, sitar or mandolin? Whatever it was, it blended well with the lantern-hung trellising, the scent of mimosa and the pleasantly numbing effect of the cool white wine.

Suddenly, Costas bounded to his feet with his arms open wide and gave a long, impassioned welcome in Greek, embracing a tall, smiling, broad-shouldered boy and, in turn, a beautiful raven-haired Greek girl with an open, trusting face. The boy embraced the tiny Mrs Costas and the equally tiny sister. Everybody embraced everybody else. With the orgy of embracing finally done, Costas brought the couple over to Dooley:

'Mr Dooley is a very fine man. English businessman. While he is here he is part of Costas family. This is my son, Theodoros. If you know Greek, it means "a gift from God".'

Dooley appraised the young man. He was disappointed to register that there was nothing untoward about him that might have marked him out as an outsider. He was handsome, courteous and had intelligent eyes. He also had the beautiful Angeliki, whom he introduced to Dooley. She was flawless with a genuine beatific smile, who presented herself for the continental air-kissing that Dooley attempted awkwardly.

The sun set quickly. Food, drink and laughter were passed generously round the table. Dooley went steady on the drink. Observation, that was the job. Theo did not look particularly like, nor unlike, his parents. It would be somewhat difficult to steer the conversation onto an appropriate line. So he watched and waited, mentally logging details. And in between he caroused with his new family and clapped in unison when Theo and Angeliki, with Theo's two cousins flanking them, performed a Greek dance which accelerated to a crescendo of handclaps, stamping feet and cheers for the simple synchronicity of wine, beauty, family, happiness and music.

He woke up the following morning wondering where he was. The early morning cicada came chattering through an open window. He looked out onto a small courtyard leading onto the track down to the town. He remembered stumbling upstairs, with Costas showing him to a room in stage whispers and barely suppressed laughter as he pointed to his own bedroom door. With a gun motion to his temple, he made the unlikely suggestion that Mrs Costas would be angry with him.

His head throbbed and the early sunshine hurt the back of his eyes. His attention was caught by a young couple walking hand in hand. The girl was in a light summer dress, the boy in shorts. It was Theo and Angeliki. They stopped near Costas' old motorbike. Dooley squinted. The boy had a mark on his left shoulder!

He quickly fetched his telephoto lens from his camera case and trained it on him. There was no doubt! It was either a remarkable coincidence or this was Patrick Bentley! They took off too quickly for a picture, the boy's long hair trailing behind and the girl gripping him tightly as she sat on the pillion seat.

Dooley was fully awake now and suddenly aware that if he played his cards right, he was a quarter of a million pounds to the good.

Breakfast on the terrace was a thick coffee and a cigarette. Costas was his irrepressibly cheerful self. Dooley engaged him in conversation about Theo, knowing that all parents are suckers for discussing their children. He learnt of his good nature. His respect for his parents. His love for his sister and cousins. He had studied hard which, allied to his natural intelligence, had earned him a place at the best university in Greece to do what he had always wanted: be an engineer and help the poor people of the lesser-known islands with their water supplies and agriculture. He had met Angeliki at college and they had become inseparable.

'They marry when they both qualify. You will come to the wedding, my friend?'

Dooley steered the conversation gently, tactfully, into seeing them that morning. After a teasing, gentle admonition about riding without helmets and "half-naked" – a real safety hazard – he mentioned, as obliquely as he could, the birthmark.

Costas smiled gently and looked out to the sea.

'It is the shape of the island. He was meant to be here. It is God's wish. That is why he is called Theodoros.'

For fear of pursuing the matter too far and appearing too intrusive, Dooley let it drop.

He visited over the next few days, insisting on photographing the bay, the restaurant, Costas and his family, Theo and Angeliki. Particularly Theo, taking care that he had several shots – it was not easy but he managed it – of the boy's birthmark. Privately, he compared it to the description in the folder. Absolutely no doubt about it. This was Patrick Bentley.

He was cautious in his email to the Bentleys:

> May have some news ... degree of uncertainty ... seeking incontrovertible proof ... returning Saturday.

You never knew who read these things, maybe hacked into them. He didn't want to prejudice his payday.

The time came for his farewells to Costas and his family. Theo and Angeliki had gone back to university, but no matter – he had the proof. The farewells took a while and Costas entreated him to come back.

'You like our beautiful island. You come back, maybe stay a little longer. Come to marriage in October. Costas will look after you.'

He turned into the long gravel drive and glanced at the portfolio on the passenger seat. Pulling up outside the mock Greco-Roman pillars. It had been a life-changing trip and now for the denouement. He slipped the portfolio into the glove box. Couldn't be too careful.

The meeting with the Bentleys was perfunctory and antiseptic. He talked about false trails and cul-de-sacs. He rendered a full account with receipts for all expenses.

'So what are you saying exactly, Mr Dooley?'

Dooley hesitated then spoke.

'I am afraid I could find absolutely no trace of the son you knew, Mr Bentley.'

He was shown politely out. He cursed himself for being so stupid as he walked to the car.

But inwardly, he smiled.

A Pretty Pickle

'Your father would have been appalled to see this level of debt. He was a valued customer of mine before his untimely death. It seems that his tenets of thrift and prudence do not appear to have been transmitted to his son.'

Murgatroyd, the bank manager administering the wigging, looked sternly over his half-rimmed glasses and dismissively slapped a schedule of debts.

'Gieves & Hawkes, tailors, £327 pounds ten shillings and sixpence. The Old Colonial Club, £189 pounds three shillings and fourpence. Pallisson & Denbow, fine vintners, £684 pounds and twelve shillings. A year's unpaid rent on No. 2, Clarendon Mews, £900 pounds … need I go on?'

Trott shuffled in his seat and shook his head embarrassedly.

'No, Mr Murgatroyd. You have, indeed, made your point. I would say, though, in my defence, that if my father had not written me out of his will, I would not be in this position.'

'Mr Trott, I have no doubt that if he had not, you would, in fact, have squandered a good deal more. At the age of 39, with no visible means of support, you seem to spend your time gambling, entertaining young ladies and drinking – only interrupted by brief interludes when you attend for waistcoat fittings!

'Well, we have now reached the end of the road. Your creditors are pressing for repayment and you have no means of satisfying their demands. Do I have to spell out what that means?'

He did not. Trott knew that discredit, bankruptcy and possibly even prison were inevitable unless he could retrieve the situation. If only those damned cards had turned over more favourably. If only his father had not settled everything on Arthur. If only that scoundrel Birkenshaw had not scuttled off with his stake of the property in the West Indies!

He trudged resignedly out of Coutts Bank, cursing his fate. He needed a plan. He needed some money. He needed a drink!

Ensconced in a booth of The Corner Pin with a glass of gin, he considered his options. Borrowing more from friends, family or the bank was worse than pointless. Getting a job was an option, but he could not immediately think what skills he could offer. Emigration? Crime? Suicide? The prospects were all too bleak.

But then his eyes widened. He smiled a private smile and quietly congratulated himself on his incisive wisdom.

That was it! He could marry money. Once married, the young lady's fortune was his by law. Result – all problems solved!

What was more, there was an ideal candidate, Alice Reynolds, more unkindly styled Alice the Heifer during ribald conversations with his low friends. He called her that to distinguish her from Pretty Alice, the barmaid at The Gaiety Public House.

Alice the Heifer was a plain, plump party in her early forties. Her father had been his father's lawyer, and he had made a handsome living from his commercial and litigation practice. The younger daughter, who had inherited the mother's looks, had been swiftly married off to a young subaltern and they lived in some style, helped by her substantial annual allowance and a regency townhouse with several servants. The elder daughter, meanwhile, languished at home, hoping for deliverance.

Mr and Mrs Reynolds had often invited him round for dinner. They kept a fine cellar and spectacular vintage ports.

After the ladies had retired, and over a glass of that fine port and a fat Cuban cigar, Mr Reynolds had hinted strongly that a Trott–Reynolds liaison would be a very desirable state of affairs.

'I know she's not in the first flush of youth and she is, like me, rather too well-disposed to pastries, but she will make some young man a sound match.' Said with a wink and a clink of glasses.

Trott had not found it difficult to resist the none-too-subtle pressure and instead indulged himself with Pretty Alice who worked in her father's alehouse, The Gaiety. Trott's own father had introduced him to the low-class delights of the dockside establishment and the respective fathers had tossed many a glass of stout back together.

Pretty Alice had her head turned by Trott Junior's flattery, his gentlemanly manners and his ability with a well-turned phrase or two. Matters had progressed, after suitable introductory outings, to regular visits to No. 2 Clarendon Mews.

'I never thought a real gentleman would pay any interest in me, Henry, but I can see that you love me and my fervent wish is that we will spend our lives together.'

Trott admitted to himself that he was very fond of Pretty Alice. Had she been more elevated, perhaps he might have acknowledged that he "loved" her. But she was a working-class girl with no fortune and rough manners. Whilst the dalliance was, shall we say, very fulfilling, she would be quite unsuitable as a wife. It would not be fair to her, as she would be laughed out of polite drawing rooms.

No, he must keep an eye on the main chance and now there was no time to spare. Once engaged to Alice Reynolds, no doubt old Mr Reynolds would be only too grateful to step in with a suitable down payment to establish the two. All creditors could be paid off and no one would be any the wiser. And – another bonus – old Reynolds himself was probably not too long for this world.

As for the marriage, there were certain formalities to go through to ensure its legality. But she was now too old for any "encumbrances" and he would be free to spend his time as he wished, at the club, playing cards, drinking fine wines and perhaps other discreet dalliances.

Trott warmed to his brilliant plan. He must formally indicate his intentions to Alice the Heifer. Then there was the small matter of Pretty Alice to finesse swiftly. There had been talk, whilst he was in drink, of marriage. She had also suggested that their complicities in Clarendon Mews seemed to have given rise to the possibility of an encumbrance, although uncertain at this point. This had spurred the talk of marriage. An illegitimate child would certainly be very unwelcome and untimely.

So that avenue must now be sealed off firmly with all haste. A breach of promise suit could be very bothersome. He must also signal his marital intentions to Alice the Heifer without further ado.

He resolved to write two letters, one to each Alice. By the end of the week all problems would be solved!

Returning to Clarendon Mews, he carefully drafted two letters. The first was to Alice Reynolds:

> My Dearest Alice,
>
> You must have been aware for some time that we have much in common. I find myself drawn to you and much admire your personality, your humour and your enviable skills in managing a household. I find myself unable to keep my feelings in check any longer.
>
> You will also know that our families share much history and I know that your father would very much wish this to continue with our generation. It is my intention, therefore, to request a private discussion with him tomorrow, to see how we may perpetuate our friendship with his blessing. I wanted to forewarn you of my

thoughts and proposals before I call on him. I have no doubt that we could foster an eminently suitable and mutually rewarding permanent relationship, and trust that I can call on your support in this proposed adventure.

My dear, may I assure you of my most ardent and fervent wishes for our future.

Yours ever,

Henry

Trott considered that this struck the correct friendly and endearing tone. Alice was almost a forgotten spinster and would jump at this last chance to be married off, particularly to an old family friend, especially one with such elan and dash!

Now for the letter to Pretty Alice. This required the right tone, firm and unequivocal, and cutting off any possible issues about children, marriage and any such preposterous notions.

After much pensive quill-chewing and a number of drafts, he was pleased with his final version:

Dear Alice,

Whilst I have enjoyed our recent friendship, I am writing formally to cancel any future arrangements. I fear that you may have read a little too much into our meetings and I feel that it is only fair to advise you that I am shortly to be betrothed to another. The latter is the daughter of an old family friend and of equivalent, if not higher, social standing and therefore eminently suitable to be my wife.

I am aware that you may have harboured aspirations of marriage and, indeed, may have misled yourself into believing that such a union may have been entertained between ourselves. However, should you aver such a thing, you should be aware that I am familiar with a firm of solicitors whose speciality, inter alia, is defamation. You should be aware that I would not hesitate to employ all means necessary.

Similarly, should your suspicions about being with child prove well founded, I will naturally defend myself against any accusations you may level. You will know that in a dispute over such a matter, the courts are more likely to prefer the word of a gentleman above that of a barmaid in a dockside hostelry, with all its various comings and goings.

Nevertheless, may I wish you well for the future. I doubt that our paths will cross, but should that happen it may be better, I am sure you will agree, if we maintain a respectful distance.

Yours truly,

Henry Trott

He read both letters again and pronounced himself satisfied. Here was an end to all his problems and a passport to the sort of life of indulgence that a young fellow deserved.

He carefully addressed the envelopes, one to Alice Reynolds of Lancaster Villas, Richmond Terrace, and the other to Alice Perkins, c/o The Gaiety Public House, Corn Mill Docks.

Summoning his factotum, Everett, he gave him instructions to deliver both letters forthwith and then allowed himself a large, cheering glass of Madeira. He resolved to call on Alice Reynolds later that day and felt assured of a rapturous welcome. No doubt there would be a certain amount of feminine frippery and he would also be required to make some appropriately affectionate noises.

All a small price to pay for a secure future.

Later that afternoon, Trott walked to the Reynolds' house, resplendent in a yellow satin waistcoat, his favourite frock coat and – to complete the picture – a silver-topped cane. He congratulated himself on his good fortune. Soon, God would be in his heaven, the sun would be in the sky and the money would be in the bank! And Mr Murgatroyd would be calling on him and giving no more of his lectures, thank you very much.

He turned into Richmond Terrace. On approaching Lancaster Villas, he noticed Alice in the window, apparently with her mother. They would be indulging in girlish delight, no doubt. Looking closer, however, it became apparent that Alice seemed to be weeping and being consoled by her mother.

On glimpsing him, her mother pointed him out and gave a shove to Alice's stout backside. The front doors opened. Trott could see Alice weeping uncontrollably, whilst walking down the path towards him.

This was most irregular!

Alice neared him, sobbing incontinently. In her hands she grasped his letter. She struggled to speak, her eyes full of tears, and – Trott noticed – her nose dripping unattractively. This was not what he expected.

She beat his chest with two small, chubby fists.

'Henry,' she sobbed. 'I can't believe it. I had no idea. It's just too incredible,' she said, waving the letter. 'All out of a clear blue sky. And I thought ...' Her voice tailed off.

A cold, vice-like hand of steel gripped Trott's entrails.

Oh God! She had the wrong letter. Somehow, in giving them a final check for tone, he had transposed the letters and she now had the one meant for Pretty Alice.

The sky had darkened. His sunny disposition had evaporated. He had to do some quick talking. This was a complete shambles. He tried to explain.

'Alice, you must understand. She was nothing. It was nothing. I never did suggest marriage to her. She's just a barmaid. And this idea that I had fathered her child, well, that's just a fantasy.

'I admit,' his words came rushing out before he could check them, 'we did have a friendship; but nothing more. The allegations are entirely false. Whatever it was is all over. A barmaid at a public house my father and I used to drink at.'

Alice's heaving bosom slowed as she listened and her eyes searched Trott's for meaning.

Then Trott had another thought. If Alice the Heifer had the letter for Pretty Alice, then the latter had one from him effectively promising marriage!

Apologising to the uncomprehending Alice Reynolds, he set off at speed to The Gaiety. This must be nipped in the bud forthwith. He would retrieve the letter and simply rip it up. That would be an end to that. His mind had not yet solved the conundrum about how to reinstate the relationship with Alice Reynolds. In his mind, he thought that might now be irretrievable.

He hurried the mile or so to the docklands and the familiar swinging sign of The Gaiety.

Somehow, he would have to circumnavigate Pretty Alice's joyful embraces, and contrive to gain access to the other letter and destroy the evidence.

He entered the dimly lit saloon. Only one or two old regulars sat silently in the low-beamed room. Pretty Alice was washing the glasses, her back turned to him as he entered. She turned and saw him. Her expression froze, then a look of pure hate contorted her features.

'What in hell are you doing here? I never expected to see you again after what you wrote. You'd better get out of here before my father comes back and finds you and goes for his rabbit gun. Get out of here and never come back!'

Trott retreated hastily in consternation. His mind raced through the permutations. So if Pretty Alice had received the correct letter after all, that meant that Alice the Heifer also had …

But those tears? Those tears were the tears of joy of a middle-aged spinster who was finally to be released from the bondage of celibate old age.

Trott let slip a long, low curse.

Every Dog Has His Day

The cold was probably the worst thing. Hunger is just another troublesome pain. One that was easily assuaged by a handful of potatoes filched from a field. Or sometimes, on good days, if you hung around certain shops at closing time, a sympathetic shop girl might slip you some food after its sell-by date. Bins were also productive. It was amazing what people would throw away – packets of unfinished sandwiches, biscuits. Once, in Hyde Park, he had chanced upon someone's discarded picnic in a Harrods bag. Quality pork pie; some Emmental cheese; chocolate. A blissful find.

If you were really desperate, you could join the shuffling queue for a handout. But those manning these refuelling stops put him off. Some were middle-class, guilt-ridden do-gooders. Some were religious types who served the soup with a compulsory slice of the Good Book. Others patronised you. The nuns were the best – an understanding smile and a whispered blessing.

Anyway, he didn't really class himself amongst the shufflers. Most were drunks. Some found temporary oblivion in drugs. There were criminals and psychiatric cases. Some were just feckless. There were social inadequates, unable to communicate. He was none of these; just a victim of some bad luck and a few wrong decisions.

Eventually, he would get straight again.

No, hunger was not really the problem. In the land of the affluent, there are always scraps for the dogs.

Loneliness could be a problem, if you let it get a grip on you. In the shiftless world in which he moved, you had to be careful about who you fell in with. But there was a certain circuit and just occasionally, there were people who helped fill those basic needs for association; a little friendliness; conversation.

There was the major. He was always immaculately turned out, with a military moustache. He carried an ancient briefcase containing a chess board and some fading army testimonials. No one really knew if he was a major, but he had a fund of interesting military stories and had been convivial company on a couple of occasions when their paths had crossed.

Joseph, a tall, misshapen man with haunted eyes, claimed to be able to speak five languages fluently and to be the possessor of a degree from Cambridge. A comment would sometimes trigger off a passage from Shakespeare or a French poem or a Latin epigram. Then his private demons, only numbed by the anaesthetising effects of alcohol, would claim him again.

He was lonely most often at those times when families should be together. The date on a discarded newspaper would remind him that it was Rosemary's birthday. He had tried to please her. He had handed over his unopened wage packet every week. He had tried to make the flat bearable. He had turned a blind eye to her little indiscretions. But her early dreams for him had faded and her feelings had soured. Who could blame her? He was only ever going to be a labourer spreading blacktop and when he was made redundant, even that meagre income dried up.

At Christmas, he would remember Janet. Little Janet skipping to the door of the flat, lisping his return. Janet, who did not mind his black fingernails and his sweat-stained boiler suit. Janet, to whom he was Dad, not some toiling no-hoper whose life turned on a business ratio calculated by an accountant with a grey suit and a cast-iron face.

Yes, loneliness was bad. But not as bad as the cold. The cold got in everywhere, despite the accumulation of tricks he had learnt. Cardboard and newspaper gave you tolerable insulation. Someone had taught him to encase his feet in polythene bags. He never removed any of his layers of clothes, on the principle that heat was retained like a night storage heater.

Finding places to sleep was an art form. The search would often begin in the early afternoon. Somewhere out of the wind, where he would not be moved on. As he travelled round, he had mapped out a series of bolt-holes. But sometimes it was not possible and he had had his share of benches, bus shelters and shop doorways. Telephone kiosks, at a push, kept the worst of the wind out, but – being lit – you were always exposed to the attentions of the circling police. Once, in some desperation on a wet, cold night, he had miscalculated the distance between towns and had slept between two cows for warmth. The beasts seemed to have understood and had tolerated the strange intruder.

It was cold today. Not the frosty, blue cold. No, it was the cold of an inescapable easterly that searched out the rips under the arms of your coat, and blew round your head until your ears were painful and your eyes watered.

*　　*　　*

70

As he travelled north, out of London, the passing traffic magnified the buffetings of the wind. A sprinkle of flickering, coloured lights testified to the season. It was nearly Christmas and the darkness was closing in early. People hurried in and out of shops into buses and taxis. They unfurled umbrellas, argued, jostled. Mothers admonished children. All proper people on purposeful missions. He watched, through a steaming cafe window, two young lovers share a kiss over a Formica table.

But he knew he was invisible to all of them, except when he was unavoidably in the way. He knew the looks of anger, fear, disgust and – worst of all – pity.

But eventually he would get straight again. He had to hold on to that; otherwise, he would slide into the abyss like all the others.

Sometimes, a passer-by would slip him a coin or two. But the good Samaritans were few and far between now.

He didn't suppose there was any reason why people should understand. They didn't have time to listen to his life story, unexceptional as it was. Anyway, they would only have told him he should have done things differently.

'So you lost your job. Lots of people do. You just get on with it.'

'The bailiffs cleaned you out? Should have gone down the social. They have handouts and loans.'

'Well, if I'd have come back and found my wife on top of some other bloke, I'd have given her a black eye, put him in hospital and sued for custody of the kid. The worst thing you could have done was fill some bags with clothes and clear off!'

Too many years had gone by now. Too many miles, too many towns, too many freezing nights. He had once been back to Chesterfield and asked Mrs Burnsall in the shop. She thought Rosemary had married an engineer and moved to Hull. Well, good luck to her. But it hurt to think of Janet calling someone else Dad. She would be sixteen now. A proper little madam, probably attracting the attentions of boys. But to him, she would always be little Janet.

He smiled a thin, reflective smile and turned his collar up against the biting wind. He was walking along one of those undistinguished and indistinguishable North London roads. He passed a bus stop. He looked up and down the road. There was no one within embarrassment distance. He didn't like people watching him delve into bins. An evening newspaper heralded: "Metropolitan Bus Strike Ends" and "Shops Expecting a Record Christmas". This would make interesting reading and later on, a little insulation.

Then there amongst the detritus of urban life, he found a cigarette packet. Always worth a quick check. Smokes these days were usually the discarded ends of hurried, unfinished throwaways. Smoking had been cheap during his army days. It had also provided an acceptable interlude between bouts of spreading blacktop. Just leaning on your shovel was idling. "Having a smoke" was a sanctified communion that no one interrupted.

He flipped open the lid. Then he closed it quickly again, with the eyes of a spaniel who had come across the Sunday joint in his feeding bowl.

The packet was full! If he didn't go at it too madly, they would last him the best part of a week. Reverently extracting one of the cigarettes, he then pocketed the others deep amongst the folds of his clothes. He always kept a dry box of matches. Lighting the cigarette, he took a long, slow, deep draught. The smoke scorched pleasurably into his lungs. The effects raced quickly round his veins and into the nerve centre in his brain that only a smoker knows about. The wind no longer felt quite so acute. If there was no real food tonight, it wouldn't matter.

He continued along the black road.

Out of the corner of his eye, he became aware of a car keeping pace with him. He didn't like to look. Maybe they were just looking for a house number. The shadowing continued for a couple of hundred yards. He pulled on the cigarette until he could no longer hold it between finger and thumbnail. He looked across at the car.

Oh God. It was a police car!

He had been pulled in enough times to know that they would not make the experience pleasant. Some aggressive questioning about some local theft … An accusation of vagrancy and a night in a cell, probably with some vomit and excrement-stained drunk …

When it happened, he always felt the indignity. Yes, he was on the road, but it was only temporary. He had had a job and a family, but things had just gone wrong. He wasn't a criminal.

Eventually, he would get straight.

He took a longer look at the police car. An unsmiling, overweight policeman with a grey crew cut was examining him. He kept walking, not wanting to antagonise. The car kept pace. Finally, it pulled up a few yards in front of him.

The electric window lowered and Grey Crew Cut made a jerking movement for him to approach. No point in doing anything else. He knew from experience that he shouldn't look in the eyes too long. That was the natural order of things. Like dogs, you had to look away first. Concentrate on the top button of the uniform. Not too furtive. Not too challenging.

'Yes, sir?'

'Where are you headed, son?'

'Up north. Out of London anyway, sir.'

He wasn't quite sure why. At certain times of year you had to get back to your origins. There was a long pause. Things were not going well. His hands tightened in his pockets. He could do without any aggravation tonight.

'I suppose you're going to haul me in?'

He looked at the police sergeant, long in experience, short on sympathy, probably looking for his quota for the night. The expressionless grey eyes appraised him for a long time. Then suddenly the face softened and the flicker of a smile creased his jowly face. He looked a different person; benign, fatherly, sympathetic.

'No, son. It's Christmas. Can we drive you somewhere?'

He frowned momentarily, unable to comprehend this ridiculous idea.

'Well,' he said hesitantly. 'I'm trying to get to the bottom of the M1. Sometimes I can get a hitch on the back of a lorry.'

'Jump in, then,' said Crew Cut, reaching round to open the rear door.

He shuffled into the middle of the back seat, expecting their attitudes to change and harden now they had him trapped. Instead the driver, a young, fair-haired, intelligent-looking man, turned round and gave him a wink.

'The sergeant's getting soft in his old age,' he said smilingly. 'Either that or the Christmas spirit has temporarily unhinged the judgement of the old bastard.'

It was warm in the car. The two policemen busied themselves with driving, answering the disembodied police radio and remaining on continuous scan for criminality on that cold, dark evening.

They dropped him off near the slip road to the motorway.

'This is your stop, son.'

He slid out of the car. The front window lowered.

'Look after yourself, son, and try to have a happy Christmas. Remember, we're not all size 12s looking for a backside to boot.'

He reached out a handshake. It was firm and friendly. It left behind a crumpled piece of paper as the window wound up and the car squealed round. He looked at the piece of paper. It was a £20 note!

This was wealth! This was security for a month. It gave him an account to draw on in emergencies. It gave him legitimacy. He could order a steaming mug of tea in a cafe and make it last an hour. He could pay for a cinema ticket and sleep in relative comfort throughout the whole programme.

He put the money into a special inaccessible pocket, along with his other dwindling treasures. A torn, monochrome snap of Janet on a donkey. A penknife he had kept since his service days. The standard, anonymised letter they had sent him when he was made redundant. The key to the flat. Mostly pointless things to anybody else. To him, they were the last vestiges of his life as a real person.

He shambled towards the bottom of the motorway. If this worked, he could sleep in the back of a lorry trundling north. If it didn't work, he'd have to find as warm a space as he could.

A queue of other hopefuls was ahead of him. Students with college scarves hitching home for Christmas. Delivery drivers with registration plates. He knew they would have preference to him. They had the open, confident body language of people with a purpose and a destination. He was a shadowy, dishevelled misfit – the type you were advised not to pick up. Still, he had his packet of cigarettes and his note for emergencies. And he might be lucky.

The wind whipped around his ankles. One or two of the hikers swept off in a flurry of backpacks, slammed doors and winking indicators.

A car pulled up. A middle-aged woman sat in the driving seat, the engine running. She would be looking to give a lift to the two clean-looking female students some 20 yards ahead. He paid little attention. No one got in. The engine kept running.

He looked across. The woman was beckoning to him. Him? His forefinger pointed to his chest and his eyebrows went up in a quizzical gesture. Was someone else approaching the car? No, she did mean him.

The window wound down and he bent to look through it. The woman leant across.

'Where are you going?'

'Err, up north; out of London; not sure exactly.'

'Well, I'm going as far as Coventry. Any help?'

'Yes, but … are you sure?'

His last comment carried an inflection which asked, 'Do you mean me? Aren't you worried about picking up deadbeats? Haven't you got this wrong?'

'Well jump in, then. That wind's keen.'

Once on their way, he darted a look at the strange woman who had dared to pick up someone like him. He looked in short, sharp glances so she would not be afraid. She was a matronly woman in late middle age, wearing glasses and with her hair trussed in a severe, no-nonsense bun.

To begin with, she made easy, aimless conversation about the weather, Christmas, the roads. As he relaxed, she began, gently, to ask him questions about himself. He answered guardedly at first, but she smiled encouragingly and warmly.

Over the next two hours, more confident now, he told her about his misfortunes, his mistakes, the problems of reintegrating with real people. Janet, Rosemary, life on the road.

She was a good listener. A genuine listener. She made sympathetic noises. She was not judgemental. He had not spoken to anyone like this for years. He thanked her profusely for giving him a lift. She could drop him off, he said, at one or two junctions where he thought he could find somewhere for the night.

Eventually, the headlights picked out the blue signs for Coventry.

'Can I offer you a hot meal at my house?'

'No, thanks. You've been very kind. You need to get home. You don't want to be bothering about someone like me.'

'But I should bother about you. Love thy neighbour as thyself. Don't worry,' she said with a chuckle. 'I'm not a religious maniac, but I do try to live by the principles. Look, you can come in, get yourself sorted and leave when you're ready. It's not charity and it's not compulsory. I live about 3 miles from here.'

He shrugged acceptance. She had a way of making it natural, friendly, easy. He wasn't going to turn a meal down.

They drove onto the concrete path of an unprepossessing, semi-detached house. They entered; she switched on the lights.

'Right, I'll get the food ready. You would probably welcome a bath. The heating's on all day this time of year so the water's hot. If you want a shave, my late husband's things are in the cabinet above the mirror. There's plenty of towels. Go on, off you go.'

She said this in a school-teacherly voice, not used to brooking any opposition, and waved him upstairs. She bustled off into the kitchen without a backward glance.

There is nothing quite like a hot bath; particularly when the cold has seared into your marrow. When you have slept, walked and lived in your clothes. When the dirty rains of London have dried on your skin and your beard begins to itch. He luxuriated in it. His lungs breathed in the clean steam.

He found the shaving things. There was a vintage badger shaving brush, proper shaving soap and a razor. He began to look human again.

Ordinarily, he did not like his reflection. Sometimes, he caught sight of a figure in a shop window. It was always a shock to realise it was him. But now, he was presentable again. He was warm. His spirits lifted.

They sank again when he turned to consider the pile of discarded, dirty clothes on the floor. A pity to put them all back on. Still, no alternative.

Some dumpy footsteps padded up the stairs and along the short corridor to the bathroom. There was a knock.

'Hello. Look, there's no point in putting all those old clothes back on. If you go into the first bedroom on the right when you're ready, you'll find my late husband's wardrobe. That stuff's been there for years. Never bothered to throw it out. Choose what you like. It's a bit old-fashioned, but it's good quality and warm. He must have been around your size.'

'Are you sure?'

'Of course. I've no use for it and he certainly hasn't now, bless him.'

When the footsteps had receded, he ventured, circumspectly, into the bedroom. Nothing had been touched for years. He guessed her husband had probably passed on in the seventies, judging by the style of clothes.

He chose, rather uncertainly, a selection of fleecy underwear, together with a thick, warm shirt, wool jumper and the trousers of a baggy brown suit. Better pick warm things. He pulled open a small top drawer, looking for socks. His eyes widened. In amongst the cufflinks and the tie pins was a gold fob watch. He picked it out carefully. It was heavy. He noted the hallmark. It was probably solid gold. He turned it over. There was an inscription on the back:

To my beloved Jack on our marriage
11 January 1961
Love Harriet.

He weighed the watch and chain; allowed the links to drip through his fingers. At a pawn shop, this would make him enough money to keep going for how long? A year? He whistled softly. It could even help him get straight again. A deposit on a small, rented flat? If he got a flat and maybe a job, perhaps Janet would come and see him.

The old woman wouldn't miss it. It must have been there thirty or forty years. Lucky it hadn't been burgled, in any case.

The permutations of what he could do went through his mind. Then, with a rueful smile, he put it carefully back in the drawer, with a confirmatory nod to himself that he was right to do so. He hadn't sunk that low yet.

He found a pair of stout black brogues. They were a size too big but better that way. He treated himself to an extra precautionary pair of socks before rescuing his few possessions from his old clothes. His treasures. His cigarettes. His note.

He went downstairs, a little ungainly in the clean, old-fashioned outfit. After knocking on the door of the kitchen, he was ushered in with a gentle stream of conversational non sequiturs.

'Come in. It's only steak and kidney pie, I'm afraid. I've been away, you see. Well, you do look a lot better. Drain those vegetables, will you? The weather seems to have passed over. It's going to be frosty. I do like to eat properly. Goodness, they're not a bad fit. I remember him wearing that jumper.'

He sat in a proper chair and ate a proper meal. A warm glow suffused his whole body. The kind of feeling you could only imagine after encountering such luxury after cold days on the road and nights sleeping rough. His hand was frequently drawn to his clean-shaven chin, enjoying the fleecy underwear against his skin. He was nearly a proper person again. She gave him a glass of wine. He tried to avoid alcohol because he saw what it did to people, but she waved away his protest. He sat in an armchair after the meal and she gave him a whisky.

'Purely medicinal, of course,' she chuckled.

She asked him some more gentle questions of his life. He felt warm. Someone was interested in him. He told her about how things had gone wrong. His shame about being a down-and-out. He told her he would like Janet to see him right now, with a clean chin, some clean clothes and drinking a Scotch out of a cut-glass tumbler! He thought about what had gone wrong. How things might have been. Maybe he could eventually get straight.

He cried softly.

She didn't seem to mind. She bustled up and fetched him another Scotch. He pulled himself together and found himself thanking her. He was thanking her for looking after him, for trusting him, for treating him as a human.

'Right, you'll sleep in the spare room. It's all made up.'

He protested, half rising from his chair.

'I'm quite happy in the ... haven't you got a shed or something ...?'

'Nonsense. Won't hear of it. Go on, off you go. You look as though you need some sleep. Old bones like mine don't. I only need four or five hours now.'

He sank into a soft bed with clean sheets and a warm eiderdown. To someone used to the unforgiving ground which numbed your hip and shoulder, or to the stealing cold which penetrated your feet, it was like falling into a bath of warm feathers. He was clean; he was full; he was warm.

The next day she gave him breakfast. She said she had relatives coming to stay; otherwise, he would have been welcome a little longer. She liked the company. No, no, she had been happy to help, waving away his thanks with mild, feigned annoyance. She had suggested a large overcoat. It was heavy, with big pockets. She asked him if he could use an old sleeping bag. Her grandson had left it years ago and it was taking up space. While you're at it, what about this rucksack? No one's had it out for years. It might as well get some proper use.

She wished him a happy Christmas and told him to call in if he was ever through Coventry again. He walked off, his spirits lifted. He was glad he hadn't stolen the fob watch.

The weather had cleared. The rain had given way to a frosty early morning. He set off towards the motorway. Perhaps he could get to Hull. Maybe, since it was Christmas, he could find Rosemary and she would let him see Janet. He was presentable. He wouldn't make any trouble. It would be nice just to see her and to wish her well and say, yes, he was doing all right and would be getting straight eventually.

The flashing light was just visible in the fog.

'We always get mist down here in this dip. And there's black ice around. Probably didn't see him. Didn't stop, anyway.'

The practised hands looked for vital signs. Not a flicker.

'Some old dosser, do you think?'

'I don't think so. He's clean and tidy enough. Mind you, these clothes weren't bought yesterday.'

He went back into the ambulance.

'Panic over. Bringing in a DOA. RTA. Casualty has no ID. No witnesses.'

He thanked the public-spirited motorist who had summoned them on his car phone and took a few details.

The police arrived.

'What happened?'

'Hit-and-run; although, it was so misty down here it would have been impossible to spot him, really. It just wasn't his day.'

They would never know.

Doing His Bit

'A lways keep your guard up,' Sergeant Major Maggs had barked at us during basic drill. 'A soldier who doesn't keep his guard up is a dead soldier.'

Johnny Tricklebank and I had heard the words but, perhaps, the brain had not received them.

Johnny and I had first met at prep school. With his fair curly hair and good looks, prowess at muddy public school games and an effortless aptitude for Greek and Algebra, he was clearly an exceptional boy. Why he chose me as his friend, I'll never know. Perhaps I played the simple, solid Doctor Watson role to his Sherlock Holmes.

But Johnny Tricklebank never suffered from the conceit of being a golden boy. He was oblivious to the admiration – no, adoration – from those of us less gifted. He had an easy grace and infectious sense of humour, to go with the charm that radiates from people who make the difficult look simple without being aware of it.

He sailed into Eton on a scholarship. I toiled night and day to scrape through. And even amongst the jeunesse dorée of our generation, his light shone brighter. He was chosen for the cricket first eleven even before he reached the sixth form. Cynical old schoolmasters would watch from the boundary and nod grudging approval as those broad shoulders flashed another square cut to the boundary. To popular acclaim, he became Captain of Cricket and Head of School.

His head was not turned by success. He would spend hours in the nets helping some young protégé to master the forward defensive stroke or spot a googly. When thanked for his help, he would simply tousle the hair or throw an imaginary uppercut with a self-deprecating laugh.

'Just you make sure you do it in the house match. I'll be watching.'

And he would be, with generous praise for the successes and unpatronising sympathy for the failures.

At Cambridge he took a first in Greats, along with a double blue. I struggled with the profundities of jurisprudence in the misplaced belief that I could become a great lawyer. I would be regularly hauled out from behind my pile of books by Johnny.

'Come on, Harold. Let's go for a punt; the sun is shining.'

'There's a ball over at Magdalen. Get your tux on.'

He would express unalloyed loyal delight over my few small successes, whilst shrugging away his own excellence in everything he tried.

One Christmas, whilst we were up at Cambridge, he invited me home for the holidays. As the train puffed away from the small Gloucestershire village station, I saw him waving from the wheel of a Bentley. He jumped out and helped stow the cases in the boot.

'Not a bad little motor,' I whistled.

'Father's runabout,' he laughed.

We raced a few miles through the frozen countryside with Johnny's gossip, questions and jokes matching the car's frantic speed. He pointed to a large sandstone house with mullioned windows, set against a rolling parkland backdrop.

'Home at last. We'll have to get some mulled wine down you, young Harold. You look frozen after that train journey.'

To my surprise, we swept past the house and along a tree-lined drive. The late afternoon orange winter sun lit majestic oaks and elms. In the distance a lake sparkled. We swept round to a gravelled terrace in front of a classic Queen Anne mansion overlooking formal gardens with ponds, fountains and statues. Away in the distance stretched prime Gloucestershire acres.

'But I thought the other house …' I stumbled quizzically.

'That's the North Lodge, you dolt. Here, help me get these cases out.'

A butler and housekeeper appeared.

'Mrs Lavery, this is my very old friend Harold Greenwood, who is gracing us with his estimable presence this Christmas. Dabbs, will you help with the cases?'

The housekeeper and butler helped with cheerful efficiency and without deference. As I was to learn later, all the staff on the estate lived in loyal security. Servants, yes, but without the rancour and churlishness that would characterise that term today. There was a symbiotic understanding between family and staff. Each knew their roles, and each valued and understood their respective places.

'I never knew you were a member of the aristocracy,' I joshed.

Johnny threw back his head and laughed at the idea.

'Well, to tell you the truth, old man, there is an "Honourable" prefix somewhere, but I can't imagine using it except, perhaps, to book a table in a particularly swish restaurant.'

The staff all clearly loved Master Johnny. Mrs Llewellyn, the pastry cook – a large dumpling of a woman evidently too much accustomed to regular samplings of her wares – would wait in concerned anticipation as Johnny tasted some new confection with the stern affectation of a wine connoisseur.

'Oh! Mrs Llewellyn. This shortbread – it's like angels dancing on my tongue!'

And she would waddle off down the stone steps to the scullery, laughing hugely and dabbing her eyes with her apron, repeating Master Johnny's latest bon mot.

But I came to understand the measure of the man, the genuine decency under the light-hearted banter, over the question of Old Pope, the gardener. General Tricklebank, Johnny's father, a stern and uncompromising man of the old school, had said that Pope would have to go. Half a century of digging, sawing, planting and hoeing in Gloucestershire frosts, winds, rain and searing sun had brought on a crippling arthritis in the man. His hands were stiff and gnarled, like the knots in an old hawthorn tree. His back was permanently bent. A problem with his hip meant the constant use of a stick.

'We'll help him find some digs in the village, but we need the cottage for a new man,' growled the General.

He was not unkind, but ran the estate with fierce efficiency. Johnny, who was increasingly assuming his hereditary responsibilities, had eventually persuaded him to take on a young lad, Roderick, to learn the job. The idea had worked. Pope bullied the young lad unmercifully. Roderick supplied the muscle, while Old Pope supplied the knowledge. Scowling under a shock of unruly hair, Roderick dug, heaved and laboured, whilst Old Pope cajoled, criticised and shook his stick at the young wastrel. But Roderick knew he was getting expert tuition, and began to learn and love the job.

When the staff lined up for their traditional Christmas box that year, Old Pope shambled forward. He had not expected to be there.

'Well, Pope,' said Johnny. 'Thank you for all your help and we look forward to many more years yet. This year there's a little extra for having to look after that young rascal Roderick and teaching him what's what.' This said with an exaggerated wink to Roderick, who grinned and blushed at his sudden fame.

Old Pope, a solitary and inarticulate man, could not let go of Johnny's handshake or find the words to express his gratitude. Dabbs stood sternly in his butler's frock coat and found he had to examine the shine on his shoes. Mrs Lavery bit her lip. A few tears rolled down Mrs Llewellyn's plump cheeks and plopped onto the apron covering her huge bosom. Johnny broke the tension by clapping his arm round the old gardener's shoulder.

'Well, that just about completes the formalities. How about a drink, old man? I think I would need one after a few months of trying to get Roderick to recognise which end of the shovel is which.'

Yes, Johnny had the undying loyalty and love of the staff, just as he had of his many friends. But there was only one girl for him. Although many admired his engaging blue eyes, his easy smile and the talents which he shrugged off, he only ever loved Alexandra. She was the black-haired, hazel-eyed daughter of the local dean. He had met her at a harvest festival dance and had told me about her whilst we were at Cambridge.

'She's the girl I'm going to marry, Harold.'

When I met her at the traditional Christmas Eve ball, I could see why. Her dark hair fell in ringlets over her shoulders. Beautiful eyes, long lashes, high cheekbones and perfectly even white teeth revealed in a ready smile, gave her uncompromising beauty. But she had an unaffected kindness and serenity to match.

They danced together at the ball as the band played in the Great Hall. Oblivious to all except each other, they swept around the floor. They made a handsome couple and were clearly so much in love. One by one, the other dancers left the floor to them and just stood and watched. The tall, fair-haired young man in his black evening suit and his beautiful, lissom dark-haired partner in a floating white ball gown. When the music finished, the spell broke. The onlookers broke into spontaneous applause. Johnny and Alexandra, who had not noticed they were dancing alone, looked around, surprised, and laughed modestly at being the unexpected centre of attention.

What pleasure, then, to be young, gifted, admired and in love. What a happy bonus also to be kind, unassuming and decent. This was the man I called my friend. Even without the title, he was, truly, the honourable Johnny Tricklebank.

The next summer, 1944, we both joined the Gloucesters. After a brief spell of square-bashing and drilling, we were both commissioned and sent off to the Western Desert. Although we were "seeing service", as the saying goes, we were in a bit of a backwater away from the front line. Once, in one of his more serious moments, Johnny had confessed that he wished he could be doing more.

'It's not that I want to be a hero and, God knows, I don't really want to kill people, but I want to do my bit. We've definitely got to finish off this evil menace, old man. Alexandra's doing her bit nursing the invalids back home. I can hardly go home to her and say I helped win the war, can I?'

And the serious moment came to an end. His eyes softened to think of Alexandra, whose picture and letters he carried. The humour returned and we lit a cigarette, and talked of home and beer and cricket.

Johnny was a captain in the Gloucesters and he led his men with those qualities which had always marked him out as a natural leader. He was always ready to listen long into the night when one of his men received a saddening letter from home. He was ready with a cigarette for those whose nerve was wavering. He would do his stint at the unglamorous jobs and lead from the front. But he did not ingratiate himself with the hardened squaddies. They recognised natural authority, decency and intelligence, and responded to it.

When we were told to do a routine desert recce one blindingly hot August day, it was Johnny who volunteered us.

'Sergeant Clark and I will lead. Harold, you and Corporal Matthews follow.'

We had set off in two light army desert vehicles. Our job was to be a routine scouting party in advance of the remainder of the brigade, who would follow in lorries carrying troops of infantrymen. We would dig in, securing the position, to be followed by supplies and artillery. The recce was in an area where the enemy was not expected to be, which is what probably induced the complacency. That, and the relentless heat and flies of the desert.

Johnny, as usual, led; driving his vehicle in the same manner that he threw the family Bentley round the Gloucestershire lanes. As far as the eye could see there was sand, boulders and the odd bush clinging precariously to life in that inhospitable climate.

As we passed over a stretch of flat ground – when I look back, it was here that we should have remembered Sergeant Major Maggs' words – I was jolted into consciousness by a huge explosion in front of us. Matthews swore and braked hard.

When the smoke and dust cleared, I looked on, horrified, as my heart thumped. I knew what I saw but I could not, for the moment, register it. Johnny's vehicle had been blown apart. Pieces of it lay in and around a small crater. The two men from inside lay some distance away. It was clear that they had been killed instantly. Johnny's body lay grotesquely twisted. I could see, through my service binoculars, the dark red blood seeping through his blond curly hair from where his face had been. I was too shocked to feel anger or sadness.

'My God! They hit a mine! We're in a bloody minefield!'

Matthews and I, acting like good soldiers and mindful now of our training, picked and inched our way over the next three-quarters of an hour to the other side of the minefield. It was obvious now where we were. The flat ground should have alerted us.

We reached rocky ground dotted with scrub and realised that we were safe. I felt guilt and shock. I could not look back. I sat on a rock and lit a cigarette. My oldest friend was dead. The nerves hit me and my hand shook as I tried to smoke. A cry from Matthews brought me back to reality.

'Sir! Look, sir; it's the rest of the convoy.'

About a mile away, a cloud of dust announced the follow-up vehicles. A couple of hundred men packed in army lorries were driving straight towards the minefield ...

'What shall we do, sir? Shall we signal?'

'They could misinterpret it,' I said grimly.

'Won't they see Captain Tricklebank's vehicle?'

'They may do, but a burnt-out vehicle is not unusual in the desert. In any case, they'll see us and make towards us. We can't risk going back.'

For a while my mind raced through the possibilities and concluded that there was little we could do except wait until they were close enough, then try to signal them to stop or turn. We watched in breathless horror as the convoy sped towards almost certain death. At least one or more of the lorries would go up, possibly triggering more mines. The few minutes that it took them to reach the edge of the minefield seemed like an hour and I felt my heart thumping in my throat.

As we watched, a strange thing happened. As they neared the minefield, the lorries slowed to walking pace. Astonishingly, they then picked an elaborate and delicate path in single file right through. They could not possibly have spotted each mine without having someone alight from the lorry and, deliberately and slowly, find and mark each mine. We had taken the best part of an hour doing just that. Someone was being reckless in driving the convoy through at that pace and would have to answer for it.

The lorries drove through to safety, drawing up beside us on soft ground. A sergeant jumped down from the lead vehicle and saluted me.

'What the hell do you think you were doing?'

'Sorry, sir?'

'Why, man, you just drove a whole convoy of lorries through a minefield at a crazy pace. Didn't you realise what you were doing? Did you realise what you were driving through?'

'Oh yes, sir, but we thought it was all right.'

'What do you mean, all right?'

'Well, sir, the young officer showed us through. He walked in front and pointed out all the mines. We thought you must have marked it all out as part of your recce.'

'What young officer? There's no one except us.' I was angry and shocked.

'Well, the young captain with the fair hair, sir. He showed us through.'

I felt my spine freeze. My breath wouldn't come.

'Did he ... did he say anything?'

'Only that he was just glad he was able to do his bit, sir.'

'Sir? Sir? Are you all right, sir?'

Drop-Dead Gorgeous

The four of us were inseparable. Fortuitously thrown together in Miss Ellesmere's primary class, we instantly made up the four corners of a parallelogram. Joined and unbreakable. In class, we fidgeted, joked, wiped noses on unravelling jumper sleeves, had spasms of contagious sniggering and – almost by osmosis – picked up the smatterings of a rudimentary education. In the tarmacked playground of a fifties gabled school we capered wildly, learned to curse, had spitting contests, sneered at the girls and were the undisputed hard cases with the other boys. Others tried to break in. They couldn't. This was my gang. The Keith Holmes' gang.

Weekends, too, were spent in and out of each other's houses, fed by despairing mothers and occasionally cuffed indiscriminately by maddened fathers, woken from a nap in front of the racing from Kempton or jostled during some painstaking surgical operation on the bowels of an old Morris 1000.

There was me, Keith. I was unofficial Godfather, planner, organiser and general corporate glue. Dave was the joker. Plump, red-cheeked, ready wit and pathological optimist. His mother said he laughed and whistled in his sleep. Danny was Mr Ideas. Bespectacled and tangibly more intelligent than the rest of us, it was him who gave shape to our otherwise shapeless time. It was Danny who designed our go-cart and invented synchronised farting. And when, later, that sort of pastime seemed somehow less hilarious, he introduced us to cribbage, fishing and the delights of sneeringly watching our local soccer team practising free fall through the lower divisions.

Then there was Hugh. Difficult to say what role Hugh played. Quietly handsome and permanently smiling, I suppose Hugh was team worker, peacemaker, diplomat, general labourer and uncomplaining butt of our malicious ribaldry. The only child of a hard-working mother – his alcoholic father had cleared off years before – he was what our mothers called "a nice lad".

'Why can't you be more like Hugh? He always offers to help out with the chores when he's around here.'

'You can go as long as Hugh's going. At least then I know you won't get into too much bother.'

If we hadn't liked him so much, we'd have hated him. Hugh was also the athletic one, the star footballer who was spotted and signed up as a youth team player with the local deadbeats.

Of course, when he left secondary school with a modest clutch of minor exam successes he also, dutifully, following the advice of his mother, got a trade. Welding apprentice. Good earnings and steady job security after five years of fetching sky hooks and grease monkeying for jokey but decent craftsmen.

After school we all went our separate ways but stayed local, meeting up at The Grapes in Devonshire Street, to chronicle the banality of our jobs and our minor successes with girls. I was an administrative nothing in the local government office. Only another thirty-seven years and an index-linked pension would be my reward for moving paper around.

Dave was a trainee salesman on the local paper. Only Dave could sell space in return for hard cash, laughing at the irony of it all. Danny … well, Danny was doing slightly better after taking a computer course at night school. He was into something called programming, which sounded pointless and unfathomable to the rest of us.

Girls? Well, we had occasional flirtations but they usually drifted away, disillusioned after failing to break into (or break up, as we saw it) the Gang of Four. Surprisingly, despite his good looks, Hugh never had a girlfriend. Despite the injunctions of our mothers for him to 'Get yourself a nice girl,' and our sardonic suggestions that maybe he lingered too long in the showers with the lads, Hugh just smiled and said that he'd know her when he saw her. Anyway, he had enough on at the factory, with the footie and helping his mum.

That is until Fay came along. Hugh was playing in the final of some local tournament. Fay was the daughter of one of the directors at the club. He had spotted her at the after-match do of sausage rolls and sparkling wine. As he told it later, unusually forthcoming for him, 'Our eyes sort of locked and something clicked in my brain.'

When we met Fay we could see why. She was drop-dead gorgeous. Thick blond hair which always fell in an attractive tumble when she ran her fingers through it. A happy face with clear blue eyes and a ready smile. A willowy body with long, athletic legs. And she laughed at our jokes! She matched us pint for pint. In fact, if the contrary evidence had not been so beautifully obvious, we would have accepted her as a bloke.

And she loved Hugh. She saw in Hugh what we did: a decent, equable, thoughtful lad and a talented sportsman. Modest to a fault, when she paid him a compliment he would, as the French say, *"balance la tête agréablement"*. A match made in heaven. The quadrangle became a pentangle but we didn't mind. And Hugh loved her, too. Of course, he didn't say that to us. Far too much of a girlie word. But he shone when she turned up cheerily in The Grapes. And he took her home to his mum, who approved of her readiness to pitch in with the washing-up and the happiness she saw in her son.

Hugh's football career flourished, too. A teenage member of the reserves, everyone predicted a bright, professional career for him. That is until one fateful, wet February night. I can see the tackle now in slow motion. A midfield gorilla called Pollock hit him from the side. We all winced. Fay looked stunned as he was stretchered off. The specialist told him the damage was irreparable and to forget football. Later on, Hugh would just pull a rueful face.

'Well, at least it's a good thing I kept up the welding.'

For some reason, after that, things didn't go so well between Fay and Hugh. They kept seeing each other, but she would make barbed comments about being a "welder's wife", except without the humour. However, blind to the change, Hugh loved her unswervingly. Then she came round less and less. There were rumours that she had been seen acting flirtatiously at other pubs and clubs. Even that someone had seen her being squired around in an upmarket sports car. Hugh shrugged at the rumours.

'She's just getting on with her life. After all, I don't own her.'

Our solicitous warnings – we didn't want our friend hurt – went unheeded. He took it particularly hard when the inevitable happened.

'I'm sorry, Hugh, but we have been growing apart, and Jeremy and I have so much in common. I thought it only fair to tell you.'

Straight out of the problem page of a woman's magazine. Jeremy thought he was God's gift. More money than you could shake a stick at and the statutory accompaniments: expensive haircut, Porsche, remote Bang & Olufson in a clinical flat. And, of course, the title. 'He's a marketing director for an international firm of property consultants,' added Fay, helpfully, as if by way of some rationale for her treachery. The fact that he was in his late thirties had either evaded her or added an air of exciting maturity.

Hugh took it hard. Dave's humour couldn't help lift him out of it. Danny tried all sorts of innovative but fruitless suggestions to focus him on something else. At least I could give him a sympathetic ear. But it was a rough few months for him.

Eventually, of course, time passed and the pain eased. It helped that Fay moved to Nice with her marketing director and that, we thought, was the last we'd hear of her. The four of us got on with our lives, going nowhere in particular but with the solace of friendship that made our humdrum jobs bearable. You can take any sort of inconsequential travail in your stride as long as you've got a six-pack, a pepperoni pizza and a video with your mates on a Friday.

For two or three years we punched a minor hole through time. Hugh got skilled. Danny got married. Dave got promoted and I got bored. Entwined like four strands of the same rope, as we had been since school.

One night Hugh came into The Grapes flourishing a letter.

'It's from her,' he grinned.

'Who?' we all asked in unison.

Fay was not any more in the forefront of our conscious minds.

'From Fay,' said Hugh emphatically. 'From France. She wants to see me again.'

He read us part of the letter. Fay whined:

> Not the man I thought he was ... doesn't pay me any attention ... never wanted to move into this primitive house ... godforsaken country ... never here ...

Hugh was unusually animated for him.

'She wants to see me. Just for a couple of days in the sun. Seems he's away at a conference and she wants me to go and stay with her.'

Apparently, she had booked a 'sweet little auberge' in a village a few miles outside Nice. She needed him. It had been so long ...

Hugh wanted to know what he should do. We looked at each other. We looked at his expectant face, his eyes shining in a way that we hadn't seen for a while.

'Well, you've got to go,' said Danny eventually. 'You really can't pass up an opportunity on a plate like that.'

We all agreed, with exaggerated winks and innuendoes. Then Hugh's face fell.

'What's the prob?'

'Well, I'll have to take time off work. That'll cost me. And it'll be a scheduled flight; probably a couple of hundred quid. I can't find that.'

We commiserated. Hugh went to get the beer in and Danny called a conspiratorial conference.

The next evening we sat looking at our beer. I fetched a clean beer mug from the bar. Hugh looked quizzical.

I pulled £80 from my pocket: 'Made a bit on the nags yesterday.' I stuffed it into the mug.

Dave put in £110. 'Sold my motorbike; crap, anyway.'

Danny put in a cheque for £100. 'Got a bit of back pay.'

Hugh looked stunned.

'Well take it, you daft sod. What are friends for? Only sorry we won't be there to watch.'

And we collapsed into our primary school giggles. Hugh pursed his lips, shook his head, smiled and raised a glass to us. We returned the gesture.

It was a couple of weeks later when the phone rang in The Grapes. Jim, the landlord, pointed the phone at me.

'It's for you, Keith. It's Hugh at Manchester Airport; seems he's back.'

The others gathered round, tugging at me for information as I interspersed Hugh's conversations with open-mouthed questions.

'So what happened, then?'

'She never!'

'So what did you say?'

And so on, until after a couple of minutes I shouted, 'Yessss!'

I made a "result" movement with my free hand then put the phone down.

The others were desperate to hear the story.

'Seems he arrived at Nice, cleared customs and picked up his bag.'

'Look, don't piss around,' interjected Dave. 'You're going to give us a guided tour of the duty-free shops in a minute.'

'I'm getting there. Anyway, they had one of those video cameras on the way out. The ones that show you who's waiting. And she was there,' I said, suspenseful. 'Hugh says that she was looking fabulous. Anyway, he gets through and sees her in the flesh, so to speak. She's blonder, more beautiful than he ever remembered, and she's wearing this clingy cotton dress. The light is shining through and you can see the outline of her.'

'You're beginning to sound like a porn script now,' said Danny long-sufferingly.

'Anyway, their eyes met, just like they did all those years ago. And they stand there. She looks a little moist and trembly. She says, "Oh! Hugh. It's been so long. I've missed you so much. I want you so much."'

'So what did Hugh say?' interjected Danny, desperate for the story to move on.

'Well, he kept looking her full in the eyes for a long time; smiling in that handsome way of his, I shouldn't doubt.'

'Yes, yes, and then what?'

'Then "butter-wouldn't-melt-in-his-mouth, too-nice-for-his-own-good Hugh" says, "Drop dead, you faithless bitch," turns on his heels and walks straight back to the next plane and out of there.'

Jim, the barman, shook his head resignedly as whoops and cheers of delight echoed around the bar of The Grapes.

Used

Roger glimpsed her through a gap in Modern Fiction. She was bending over one of those little trolleys they used to return books. Her long auburn hair fell forward as she retrieved and replaced each book. Vainly, she tried to stow it behind her ears. She had a cardigan thrown round her shoulders in the way that librarians do.

Expertly, Roger appraised his quarry. He could see her outline through the clinging print dress which finished just below her knees. The hips were womanly, but not too wide. Just how he liked them. The shape of her buttocks was round and firm. Her calves, ankles and gathered waistline told him that there was no excess flesh on her – just enough to make her soft and welcoming and interesting.

She moved her trolley round to Autobiographies. Roger followed her surreptitiously. She had that slow, swinging gait that testified to long, lithe, athletic legs. Her hips moved enticingly under the dress. Roger imagined her naked, walking towards the light of a bathroom, her hair tumbling down over soft shoulder blades to the slim waist, with the pear-shaped hips moving in the way that only a woman's hips moved.

He padded round to Modern History to keep her in view. He was not obvious about it. He had done this before, in art galleries, in supermarkets – even, once, at a church jumble sale. He positioned himself so that he had her in full view at a glance, whilst purportedly examining books on World War Two.

He was not prepared for what he saw. She bent over to pick up several volumes. The top button of her dress was open. Her beautiful round breasts hung, pendulous, against the fabric. He could see from the deep valley and the swing of them as she picked up and replaced books that they were magnificent. No droop there. When she stood erect they were uptilted, straining through the fabric.

And her face! She was strikingly perfect. Arched eyebrows, high cheekbones, perfect green eyes and the clean sweep of an aristocratic chin line down to a slim neck. Her mouth pressed in concentration as she searched for the appropriate perches for the books. Her long fingers languorously stroked the binding of one particularly recalcitrant volume. She was beautiful, she was physically perfect and she had that relaxed, confident, intelligent bearing that suggested breeding and self-possession.

She looked at him momentarily. Someone who is being watched, however circumspectly, will eventually feel the weight of eyes upon them, particularly eyes that are devouring what they see. Roger held his gaze and smiled a faint smile of acknowledgement. She did not reciprocate, but modestly averted her eyes to carry on with her task.

He had the feeling that this was going to be a challenge, but one which was well worth pursuing. He watched her return to the checkout desk, busying herself with removing cards, stamping books, giving directions to enquiries and entering information into the computer. Her movements were restrained. Not for her that obvious brassy, bosomy bounciness that advertised the insolent self-confidence of a woman who knows she is being watched. She was quiet, demure, modest ... even – Roger caught his breath a little – virginal? Perhaps here in this backwater of a library, in a job not renowned for extrovert types, life and love had passed her by. She probably lived with her mother nearby, went to church, read books, of course, maybe did a little cycling and walking.

Roger sucked his teeth at all that sensuality waiting to be unleashed. He picked two or three pulp fiction potboilers and waited until the odds were that she would deal with him. He hitched up his clothes and ran his fingers through his hair so that it would appear to best effect. He was proud of his hair; thick, straight and blond, which fell appealingly over a handsome, open face. His looks certainly helped. He was also pleased personally with his engaging conversation, showing interest in women and making flattering – but not too obvious – personal comments. To complete his personal attractiveness, he had the customised sports car. That always impressed. It cost him a fair proportion of his salary, but it had more than paid its way in the past.

He kept his eyes on her while queuing. It was important to establish optimum eye contact. The first, accidental collision had not helped. He had to retrieve the situation. She dealt expertly with his books, her head down, absorbed in the task. He ran his eyes over her. Her hair hung forward as she bent over the desk. A slight hunching of her shoulders allowed him to see a short way down her back. There was an attractive freckle which went with her auburn colouring. He could hear the rustle of that firm body moving within the dress. She did not look at him. He had to establish contact.

'Are any of these any good?' He laughed a little nervously.

She looked up, a little surprised. She studied his face momentarily. He crinkled his eyes to demonstrate good intentions. She looked down again without smiling.

'I don't know. I haven't read any of them.'

Then she was on to the next customer. He had no alternative but to pass on through the turnstile and out into the slightly chill air of an early April Saturday morning. He could see the back of her as he passed the window. He blew his cheeks out and widened his eyes to himself, acknowledging that here was, indeed, a worthy prey.

Of course, he did not think of them as prey. He was a giver, a sharer, an educator, helping girls reach their full potential. And if there was something in it for him, well, that was a bonus. That was not how his friends viewed him and to be honest, he quite enjoyed his rather risqué reputation. In the back-slapping, barking, lewd circle of friends in the pub, he was referred to as 'Roger by name and Roger by nature.'

He had to admit, there had been quite a few women. He enjoyed the chase most of all. Although there was a certain frisson when they gave one of those little gasps that he liked so much, he knew – from that point on – the magic had gone. He had developed all sorts of artifices to get to that point of no return: the point where they were putty in his hands. There was the little-boy-lost approach, which appealed to the most dominating woman. The confident man-who-has-seen-it-all-before usually pulled in the shyer, more reluctant types. Some, of course, you had to romance; dinner usually did it. For very self-confident women, it was fascinating for them to believe he was not interested in them. Not until it was too late, anyway.

He prided himself on structuring the approach to the individual. They were all different, but really they were all the same. Occasionally, a particularly pretty one had lasted a week or two. It was wrong, however, to get too emotionally involved. Your judgement went. Anyhow, what was that saying that his mate Flick liked to quote?

'So many women. So little time.'

As he stirred his coffee in the little cafe he frequented – you could see the talent out doing its shopping – he ruminated on the required approach. Asking her out directly would be too obvious and guaranteed to fail with a shy girl like that. No. He had to appear normal, friendly. A familiar face. There must be a natural progression. He had to find out what her interests were. Yes, that was it. He could accidentally bump into her somewhere once she recognised him. He could take it from there. At that point he would be on autopilot and it would only be a matter of time.

Roger's eyes idly followed the girl who cleared away the cups, plates and half-finished breakfasts. Below conscious level, he categorised her as a vague possible. It was definitely a womanly shape, but the blue nylon overall and the dyed black hair and heavy mascara were a little off-putting. Similarly, his eyes followed a few women passing the cafe window. The duration of his gaze equated to the level of attractiveness.

An older woman, thick in hip and thigh, and with the telltale signs of age beginning in an otherwise pretty face, merited only a brief glance. A pretty face in a shapely body was followed, with a flicker of attention to all the important bits, until she disappeared from view. But his heart was not in it.

Over the rim of his coffee cup, a picture kept running. A picture of her in profile: pink tongue playing in concentration along pretty lips; slim, young fingers stroking a book; the curve of her young breasts, hips and calves, accentuated by a stance on slight tiptoe as she searched for reference numbers. He had to have her!

He thought about the current stable. There was Jennifer, a secretary from work: pretty but stupid. She had only required a couple of assignations at the local pub before she capitulated. She was keen on him, he knew, but after only two or three encounters he was already bored. Alison was useful occasionally. A teacher with a flat in town, she was desperately lonely. When he rang her up, she cleared the decks whenever he wanted to visit. About once a fortnight was satisfactory, but he couldn't stand those big, calf eyes in the morning, asking him when he would be back. Deborah was a student at the local college he had met at a discotheque. That had to stop now. She was dangerous. All that talk about giving up her course, moving in with him and having children spelt disaster if he let it run any further. Anyway, she had served her purpose. He resolved to end things with both Jennifer and Deborah. Alison he would keep as a backstop in case of eventualities. As long as she didn't make any demands or suggest things got complicated.

The following Saturday, Roger's careful strategy began to be put into operation. His visits to the library became more regular. He took to selecting "improving" books – on mythology, travel, the Classics – hoping that she would notice and be impressed. He managed to choose times when the library was not busy and had exchanged a few words with her.

Once, he thought he noted a flicker of interest. Then two strokes of luck aided him in his quest. First, the library decided, in an attempt to be customer-friendly, to issue name badges to their staff. He knew now that she was called Flora McInerny. By dint of elimination, he had established her address from the pages of the telephone directory. A couple of judicious wrong-number phone calls suggested that she did, indeed, live with one other older woman. The age of the voice and the gentle Edinburgh accent could only mean that this was her mother, as he had suspected. A request to speak to Mr McInerny elicited the response that there was no one there of that name.

Then, by chance, he had seen a small ad in the local paper for a talk at the English Speaking Union:

> Flora McInerny will present a talk on the nineteenth-century English novel at the Jubilee Hall, Washington Road, on Thursday, 27 May, at 7.30 p.m. New members welcome. Light refreshments.

He had presented himself at the dilapidated, shabby church hall on the specified date. He had looked slightly out of place amongst the mainly middle-aged and middle-class members as he sipped a polystyrene beaker of tea, dispensed from an industrial-sized tea urn. He sat, entranced, on one of the hard wooden church hall chairs.

He neither understood nor remembered a word of the presentation. He watched her, somewhat blushingly and nervously, read what was obviously a prepared text containing a lot of words, phrases and names that he had not previously encountered. He liked the way her free arm folded across her chest, although occasionally retrieving a strand of the straying, long auburn curls. Just now and then her tongue would lick dry lips. She balanced on the outside edge of one foot like a schoolgirl being told off in the headmistress' study. She was absolutely bewitching. From the safety of his seat, his eyes ran lasciviously up and down her body. He imagined her running away from him along a deserted beach, being laughingly caught, then yielding quietly, seriously, moistly, but willingly, to his urgent, searching fingers.

At the end of the presentation, he ventured to speak to her as she stood with tea and digestive biscuit amongst a group of politely interested bystanders. He established that she was, indeed, Flora from the library.

'I never knew you were such an authority.'

'Oh! I'm not, really; it's just an interest. Goes with the job, I suppose.'

She was sweet; vulnerable; succulent. He switched on every ounce of attention.

The others began to melt away, sensing a conversation that had begun to exclude them. He managed to fend off any questions concerning his rather surprising attendance there. He deftly handled a gentle enquiry about the depth of his knowledge of nineteenth-century literature. He focused his charm. He established a lot of eye contact. He smiled encouragingly. He even gently touched her arm to move her away as someone passed them to leave. He was making progress! She was responding to him!

As a brown-overalled functionary meaningfully stacked chairs, noisily signifying that it was time for them to leave, he decided to make a move.

'Listen, it's still quite early. Do you want to go for a coffee or a drink or something?'

'No, thank you very much. I have to get home. Mother will be expecting me.'

Damn! He should have thought before making such an early move. She was not one of your checkout girls or secretaries who expected an obvious, full-frontal approach. She had class. Like a classic horse that had not yet been broken in, she must be handled gently but firmly. These things take time.

'Oh, well. Probably see you in the library, then. I'll get you to recommend something,' he laughed.

'Yes, I'd be happy to.'

Formal but nevertheless much warmer. It had taken three or four weeks and a lot of effort, but he was getting there. She mouthed a silent, smiling goodbye as she pulled her coat down from the row of brass hooks and hurried into the darkening spring evening. He knew, from long experience of picking up signals, that it was now just a matter of time. He had felt the lust rising in him as he spoke to her. It had taken a supreme effort of will not to stand too close and not to savour her skin, her scent and her contours.

As he walked home, he imagined unhooking her bra and watching her breasts spring free. He mentally ran his hands down the small of her back to her hips as she rested her cheek on his shoulder, her eyes closed. He was aroused. He found a telephone kiosk and dialled Alison. Excitedly, she agreed that, of course, he could come round.

Events moved Roger's way. He developed an interest in literature, taking care not to get in too deep conversationally. He professed an interest in the Lake District; although his only recollection was a series of gritty pubs, these seen through an alcoholic haze on a youth-hostelling tour with some of his low friends. Chameleon-like, he moulded his character, his clothes, his conversation and his interests in order to ingratiate himself with her.

It began to work. They walked round the pond in the park one lunchtime and Roger fed his sandwiches, magnanimously, to the ducks. As he chanced to be in the library at closing time on one occasion, he walked her home. She accepted his offer of a coffee one Saturday lunchtime. Then, casually, he said that he had been given two tickets to the local theatre to see *Bleak House*. Would she, by any chance, be interested in going along? She was delighted and also smiled very approvingly at his suggestion that they might grab a bite to eat afterwards.

*   *   *

The evening went better than he expected. During the play, he held her hand and his forearm rested on her thigh. Over an intimate dinner, there was more hand-holding and eyes locked in wordless smiles full of meaning. She drank most of the bottle of red wine, as Roger insisted he was driving. As long as he was measured and did nothing to startle this beautiful young fawn, he would eventually, he was certain, be running his hands and mouth over her naked skin. Perhaps not tonight, but soon.

When he suggested in the car that they might go back to his flat, his heart thumped when she whispered a smiling, 'Yes.' He could feel the desire in his throat and loins as she walked in front of him up the stairs to his flat. It had taken some time and a deal of concentrated effort, but he was now within sight of his prize.

Once in his own territory, he slipped methodically into his usual plan. He let her get the feel of the flat. She wandered around looking at photographs, books and his music collection. He busied himself with coffee in the narrow kitchen, watching her through the open door. She looked relaxed. She slipped off her coat and threw it over the back of a chair. She let her finger drag along the back of the sofa as she casually walked round. Her hair was tied back with a ribbon and in the dim lighting, she looked beautiful, physical, graceful and sexual.

He had been right. Here was a woman waiting to be unleashed. It was beginning to look as if his careful courtship, the wine and, of course, his own unfailing charm had worked to good effect. He cautioned himself. Don't rush it, Roger. Don't blow it tonight by being too hasty. A girl like that is going to take fright if you are too forceful!

He brought in the coffee. Very subtly, he managed to get close to her on the sofa. His arm stole round her shoulders. They talked. They laughed. He kissed her: a chaste kiss, fleetingly, on the lips. She responded. There began to be more physical contact. His hand tentatively brushed her breast. He could feel the nipple hard through the material. She drew back suddenly.

'Roger, I'm not sure.'

'It's all right. It's all right,' he soothed. 'I'm not going to try and make you do anything you don't want to.'

She seemed reassured by this and allowed further intimacies. She began to breathe heavily. She made her body available. There was no further protest when his hand expertly slid along her warm thigh. She breathed his name. Her breath was sweet. Her eyes were closed. Roger knew that the signals were now unmistakable.

He took a risk in standing up and leading her to the bedroom. But he had played these percentages before. It was now, however, a question of when, not whether. If she hesitated at the door, he could revert to the sofa with reassurances. If it meant the end of the opportunity this evening, it was certain next time.

She did not hesitate. As he closed the curtains, she began unbuttoning the front of her dress. He turned and watched as she fixed him with a loving look. She stepped out of the dress, turned down the bedclothes and elegantly climbed in. Roger sat on the bed stroking her beautiful, long hair as she lay there looking a little uncertain. He kissed her and pulled away a little.

'You know, we've only known each other for a short time, but already I think I'm in love with you.'

He knew that would be the clincher. She enveloped him. He turned off the light. It was an ecstatic night. Cool, soft skin in contact with hard skin. The smell of a young, clean, pure woman's body. Yielding moistness; firm, long legs arching her body towards him. A period of quietness, then a resurgence of bodies. Fingers, fingernails, tongues. Skin to skin. Mingled hot breath. He had never had a night like it. He was giving her more pleasure than he dreamed possible. He was freeing her emotions which had lain dormant for so long. His own pleasure, of course, was almost incidental. He was happy to be able to tutor her in these physical skills. She was an eager learner.

In the morning, as the half-light filtered through the curtains, she slid out of bed just as he had imagined. She walked, naked, towards the bathroom. He saw her silhouette as she switched on the light. Her hands pulled her hair together behind her head, lifting her breasts. She half turned and gave him a smile. God, she was lovely – and he'd just had a night of her. He was a lucky bastard. Now the ice was well broken, he could play it as he wished.

She came out of the bathroom rubbing her wet hair, now encircled by a towel fastened under the armpits and finishing halfway up her thighs. He watched her and felt himself stirring again.

'Come over here,' he said in a low monotone.

She came over and kissed him briefly, resisting his attempts to pull her back into bed.

'I have to get to work. I'm going to be late.'

She quickly dressed, bent over and kissed him perfunctorily again. He grabbed her wrist.

'When am I going to see you again?'

She smiled. 'You know where I am.'

She left quietly. He lay back in the bed, his arms folded behind his head. He congratulated himself on his tactics. He knew about women. Now, she would want to remain involved and he could fit her in as and when he wished. However he must, he mused, play her along a little, just to let her know. What did Flick say?

'Treat 'em mean, keep 'em keen.'

He didn't ring her for a week. Neither did he go to the library. He spoke to his circle in the pub about her. There was much ribaldry. Elbows were dug into his ribs and eyebrows raised suggestively.

'So, when are you going to have your wicked way again?' leered Flick.

'I'll go and see her today. Tell her I've been busy. I fancy another slice now. God, she's lovely. Actually, she's rather a nice person, too.'

This attracted accusations of Roger going soft and breaking the code. In order not to appear as though he was weakening, he joined in with the lewd posturings and aggressive drinking; but he silently considered that it was time to get in touch. She had probably suffered enough. If he let her stew any longer, it would not make her keen. It would have the reverse effect: she would get frosty. Anyway, he liked her. It was all a question of timing and it was important not to misjudge. Besides, he wanted to be running his tongue down that flat stomach and to watch her close her eyes and ...

'Sorry, chaps. Have to go. Catch you on Saturday.'

It was early afternoon. On his way to the library he passed a flower shop. Sheepishly, he bought a small bunch of tulips and freesias. He felt even more sheepish carrying them into the library, but they were a useful insurance policy, just in case he had left it a little too long. He looked through the window of the library. Good, she was on her own, over by the computer. Don't want anyone I know seeing me give a woman flowers.

He went in and made his way over to her workstation. He thrust the flowers towards her and smiled.

'Hi. I've missed you. Sorry, I've been a bit err ... tied up.'

She looked up briefly from the keyboard and smiled; a mechanical smile that did not extend to her eyes.

'Oh, hello. Oh, thank you for the flowers. Sorry, I'm a bit busy myself right now.'

She put the flowers on a side table and gave him a little smile which terminated the exchange.

'Any chance of meeting up tonight? We could go out for a meal, pictures, back to my place – up to you, really.'

'I have a meeting tonight. Perhaps another time.'

Oh, God, he had blown it! He didn't normally get these things wrong. He should have phoned at least. She was not like the others. She was obviously an inexperienced girl and the other night had quite clearly represented a huge commitment on her part. He had missed that part in his calculations.

'Look, I'm sorry. Can we be friends?' He knew the chill atmosphere must be thawed right now.

'Of course we can. Give me a call sometime.'

This evidently was her last word, as she set about the computer keyboard furiously, paying minute attention to the figures and symbols.

Roger left and silently cursed himself. He had been stupid and mistimed it. She would have felt cheap; used. He could retrieve the situation, but it would take some time.

He wanted her again. Another emotion. He did not articulate into conscious thought, but he was also aware that he was feeling something a little deeper. She was clearly a different dimension to the others. He could be persuaded to be quite serious about this one. Still, he could pull it back. It just required a bit of charm; a bit of effort.

She needed to know that he was serious, a regular guy, even – he winced a little to admit it to himself – prepared to be serious about this. She would be back naked in his bed within a fortnight, he promised himself, walking towards the cafe.

Marjorie came over from Returns. A plump girl of indeterminate age, she was fascinated by the human interactions of the other librarians. She secured surrogate satisfaction from hearing of the human condition – arguments, emotions, sexual encounters – from others. She also enjoyed retailing particularly spicy snippets to willing ears.

'What was that all about? That bloke with the flowers.'

'Oh, that was Roger. Went out with him last week. I suspect he's going to be a little troublesome.'

'I've seen him in here before. You played him along a bit. Why do you do that?'

'Makes them keen. Usually get a better performance out of them. Roger? Well, only six out of ten, really.'

'You are naughty. Are you going to see him again?'

'Roger? No. I got what I wanted. I'm not ready for anything more involved. Anyway, Marjorie, what do you think about him?' she asked, lowering her voice and nodding towards a young dark-haired man examining books in Philosophy.

Chance in a Million

He had become an expert at trawling the Internet dating sites. Not too young – fifty-plus was ideal. And he could spot the signs of vulnerability:

My first time trying this; recently divorced but looking to start again; happy to hear from anyone – age immaterial. Prepared to travel anywhere for the right individual.

So the profile of Beryl Bartley was almost an open invitation:

I am just the wrong side of fifty but still considered attractive. I have never been married as I have had to care for my mother, who sadly passed away a year ago. I recently went to a wedding of an old friend of mine who met her man online and they are blissfully happy. She encouraged me to try, so what have I got to lose!

I live in a quiet market town in Middle England and have my own house and car, and work in local government. I'm looking for the man of my dreams, so if you're out there, George Clooney, get in touch immediately! Seriously, I'm hoping to meet someone who is between forty-five and sixty. Preferably above average height and who looks after himself. You're likely to be a professional of some type and, like me, you don't think you should be doing this, but don't do discos any more! If you're single like me – fine; but happy to meet if you are divorced or widowed.

My interests are walking (you have to like dogs!), swimming, dancing, eating out or in, theatre, cinema and antique shops. My friends say I am quite stylish and feminine but have a wicked sense of humour!

It would be good if you lived close, but if we turn out to be right for each other, then distance isn't a problem.

Maguire looked at the picture. Plain; a slightly awkward smile; standing in front of a view, in an anorak, with a spaniel at her feet; probably cropped from a rambling-club outing.

Perfect.

Maguire gave himself a small, congratulatory smile. He looked at the date the profile was first posted. Quite a while now – four months – excellent. Chances were that she had had a few unsuitable responses or – possibly – no response at all. Maybe becoming a little disillusioned with it all now, and only half-heartedly checking the site and wondering whether the sign-up fee was worth it.

Maguire slipped into his well-practised routine. This would be like shooting fish in a barrel. He considered all the personas in his portfolio. Maybe Mike, the US soldier in Afghanistan, divorced father of one. Or maybe Alan, the airline pilot, with his very demanding job that required him to be constantly on the move. No, this needed an amalgam of fictional people.

Beryl typed in her ID and password. Gracious! A reply! And he looks very presentable. A rugged, broad-shouldered man in army combats smiled an open smile in a desert scene. Alongside was a picture gallery with snaps of the same man with two panting Labradors and a picture of him in running kit in a race of some sort.

> Hello, my name's Chris. No doubt you've had all the biographical stuff we have to complete, but thought I would fill in the picture.
>
> I saw your profile and picture and felt an instant attraction. I'm fifty-three, but try to keep myself fit and active by walking my dogs and jogging – as you can see from the photos. I'm also fairly recently bereaved, my wife passing away a couple of years ago. I keep myself busy with work and friends and travel – displacement activities, I guess, but I feel that it's now time to strike out again in life, and I'm sure that's what she would have wanted.
>
> I'm originally from Reading, which is still my base in the UK (is that anywhere near you?), but work as a construction engineer, project managing developments around the globe. Currently I'm in the States, working on a sports stadium in Cincinnati. I'm missing home (!) and my dogs Dolly and Daisy (see picture), who stay with friends when I'm away.
>
> Hopefully after this job I'll get a home billet back in dear old Blighty, and I can settle down and slow up a bit. Feel as though I've been tearing around for years having been a captain in the army,

102

Royal Engineers, which is where I learned my trade. Hence, by the way, the desert scene: the most flattering picture I could find!

So that's me: international nomad. I've lots of friends but a bit short on family. I was an only child, my parents passed away some time ago, and Daphne and I were never blessed with kids. So, all the more reason to look for someone who is my kindred spirit, fellow red wine drinker and general partner in crime!

My interests: similar to yours. But you should also know that one of my great passions in life is for wildlife. When I can I run marathons (picture!) for a couple of charities I support – a seal sanctuary in Cornwall and a home for retired donkeys in Andalucía. I've been fortunate to visit both and I give my time and money to help where I can. Well, that's me. When I pressed my friends to describe me after telling them about this (they all laughed like drains!), they came up with "kind, happy, responsible citizen". And then they told me to find someone quick because they are fed up with me being the odd singleton at dinner parties!

Beryl, I do like the sound of you and I hope that you may feel something similar for me. It would be wonderful to get a reply but – even if you don't – may I wish you all the luck in the world with your search. You seem like a lovely person who deserves somebody good.

Best wishes,

Chris (Christopher Leftley-Smith).

Maguire liked the last part and also the fact that he had invested the character with a double-barrelled, solid name.

Beryl thought promising, very promising, and tapped out an instant answer:

Chris,

Very good to get your profile and pictures. I'm surprised a man like you hasn't been snapped up long since. Yes, it does seem that we do have a lot in common. And I bet Dolly and Daisy would love to meet Cinders, my springer spaniel. Yes, Reading is less than an hour away from me. And my father, bless him, was also in the army like you and he saw service in the Second World War. Then, believe it or not, one of the charities I support is the World Wildlife Fund – so "check" again!

I was sorry to read about your wife. You must miss her very much. But, as you say, life goes on and every journey starts with a single step. And you've made the first step by being brave enough to write in response to my profile.

It would be wonderful if we could meet – when are you next in the UK? But I hope if we do you won't be disappointed. I'm not the femme fatale-type; just a reasonably attractive homebody looking to find that one special person before too much of life passes by. Hope to hear again from you soon.

Love and best wishes,

Beryl

Maguire smiled. The bait had been taken. Now just leave it a couple of days before replying. That way, the target thought their ideal correspondent had lost interest or found another more interesting profile. Ramp up the emotional investment.

It was four days before his reply:

Hi, Beryl,

So sorry not to reply sooner, but it's been ferociously busy here at work and I've been snowed.

I have spent some of the time looking at your picture. I printed it off and keep it in my wallet. Strange, isn't it, how you can feel an instant attraction and affinity with some people? But there is definitely something about your look and what you have told me about yourself that makes me strongly attracted to you.

I wish I was back home right now and could go walking with you and the dogs and chat all the way round. But the project is at a critical phase and I can't get away. Also, the client here seems to be in some financial difficulties and all accounts have been temporarily frozen, including my own personal account! Seems to be something to do with the law over here – companies and principals or something. Oh well, it's takeaway pizza not steak for Chris at the moment!

Although we've only been talking to each other for a very short time, it's good to know that maybe there's someone out there on my side and keeping the home fires burning, so to speak. I guess I am still a little vulnerable, too. It's only a comparatively short time since Daphne died. But I do think – chance in a million, I guess – somehow we may have found what we are both looking for. The Next Step.

I do get a little down. The proprietor of the hotel is threatening to dump me and my bag on the sidewalk unless he gets paid! But I smile and think of England and sitting down with you in front of a roaring fire with a glass of something nice, talking about the future. Wonderful dream.

By the way, why don't we move on to regular email, rather than through this website? So much quicker and direct, and you also won't have to pay any more subscriptions. (I guess I'm secretly hoping, too, that there won't be any other guys trying to take you away from me!)

My email address is chrisl-smith@sweetmail.com. By the way, we could also talk direct. My mobile number is 07941 682115. But remember, it's a six-hour time difference over here.

Hope to hear from you soon, sweetie.

Kisses,

Chris

x

A couple of days later, Beryl replied by email:

Chris,

It was wonderful to have such a long chat with you yesterday, even if I did get the time zone a bit muddled up. I never thought that at my age I would ever meet someone like you. I thought all you men went for younger women. But I loved hearing your voice and all about your life and work. We truly do seem to have made a magical connection.

I have a small confession to make. My friend told me I have to be so careful about people I meet on the Internet, so I checked out your Facebook site. If you look, you'll see you have a new friend! But that only underlined what I thought – what a handsome, kind, intelligent, thoughtful man. And I told my friend Evie I've now checked you out via email, phone and Facebook. She was so pleased for me and likes the sound of you.

Then, that poem you had found and read to me – well, it really made my heart melt. I just wish you were here with me right now to give me a big, manly hug and tell me what you told me on the phone.

How did this happen! It's only been a week or two but already I feel as if I've known you forever. But I think we also know that it is so right and that we can start planning for the future. We're so lucky.

I was anxious to hear about your short-term financial problem. It isn't right that they get you all wrapped up in their wranglings over the development. After all, you're only trying to do the job as best you can. If there is anything I can do, let me know. I'm very solvent, particularly after mum died, and we've now sorted probate and sold her house. So let me know if there's anything I can do and *don't be shy of asking*!

But most of all, darling, (I hope you don't mind me calling you that – so forward!) keep your spirits up and keep thinking about me and how we'll be together soon. I know I do. I daydream about you and thank my lucky stars for the happy coincidence that we met when we did.

All my love,

Beryl

xxx

Maguire read the email with quiet satisfaction. It was all going perfectly. He had had to do some quick thinking on the phone, but a practised professional like him had covered virtually every base beforehand. Nothing he couldn't handle. And didn't they all go for the poetry? How many times? How many desperate, gullible women?

Still, she had plenty of cash and it was only fair that she could now recycle some of it in his direction. Maybe he could donate a slice to a donkey sanctuary! And his aspirations of a few grand had suddenly rocketed. If she was sitting on a cash pile, including proceeds from a house sale and a will, he mused that, maybe, we were now talking about big, six-figure numbers. So confidence must be instilled. Care must be taken. Mustn't frighten the target before the kill shot. But there could soon be a very big payday!

He emailed her back:

Hi, Beryl – or should I say "darling"?

Yes, I think I will. Good to talk to you on the phone again last night (my night). Crazy, isn't it, how much we have in common? It's been a long time since I felt like this, so let's just go for it.

> You put a spring in my step,
> a smile on my face
> and a twinkle in my eye.
> I'm a long way away,
> but I can't wait for the day
> when I can get away from this
> misbegotten project and come back to England
> to see the woman I want to spend my life with.

Magical connection, indeed! I can't remember what my horoscope said for the month of July, but whatever it was it could never have matched the miracle that happened. There is so much more I want to say to you and so many places to go. So many things we can now plan together.

Anyway, some bright news. The lawyers on the job successfully argued that my personal finances should be excluded from the aggro over the commercial contract. So I've got my money unfrozen and can pay my personal bills, including the motel bill, much to the satisfaction of Raoul, the manager, who was beginning to get a bit heavy. So I think a beer tonight for Leftley-Smith! And I'll raise my glass to the east, towards the woman who has captured my heart. But thank you, anyway, for your very kind offer.

Seems, too, that someone, despite all the financial jiggery-pokery, is going to make a bit of a killing on this job. It's all been a bit of a dog, but it will turn out OK, I'll make sure of that. Apparently, one of the consortium dropped out because of cash problems and his stake – about $300,000, I think – is up for grabs. Trouble is, no one will touch it because they think it's going to make a loss. But, as the project director with his finger on the pulse, I've seen all the financial forecasts, the cash-flow projections and completion plans. Whoever piles in with that money is going to make treble their investment within three months, when the job is scheduled to finish. Just wish I had the spare readies. The other consortium partners are already leveraged up to the eyeballs and, in any case, don't yet know what I know.

Oh, my darling. There I go talking shop when I should be talking about you, me, us, Dolly, Daisy and Cinders walking along the banks of the River Severn on a glorious autumn evening on our way to The Angler. Don't suppose you know it, near Henley? Well, only a couple of months and I'll be there. I can't believe it.

So, think of me when you snuggle up in bed tonight. I don't need any encouragement to think of you. My problem is keeping my mind on this job as I close it out. But the wait will make it all the sweeter. I hope you'll come and meet me at the airport and that maybe you can book a couple of days off work; then we can spend those first few days together, just you and me (and the dogs!).

All my love,

Chris

x

Beryl wasted no time in replying:

Darling Chris,

Been thinking about you lots, working hard over there. I'm glad you've got your money unfrozen. At least you can eat properly.

I've been doing some thinking about what you said. Why should someone else get the benefit of your hard work? Surely you are entitled to get a share of the rewards after all you've done. So maybe – and don't shout me down on this until you've given it some serious consideration – I can provide the money. It's all sitting in an account with the solicitor at the moment and I've been wondering where to put it to get a good return.

Somehow National Savings, bank deposits and cash ISAs aren't very exciting. By the time I've paid tax on it and the government has had its slice, it will hardly make a ripple. If we can triple the value in a few months, just think what it could do for us. You can take a job nearer home. We can have the holiday of a lifetime and we'll have security in the bank for our future together. Don't dismiss it! Think about it. Maybe this was meant to be, too!

Whatever you decide, you know that I am with you all the way. I love your idea of a walk by the river. Funnily enough, I know The Angler. My dad used to take us there when I was a little girl. I sat on a bench as dusk fell and watched the trout rising for mayfly. Another weird connection we have. Isn't that spooky?

Of course I'll come and meet you at the airport. Just hope I don't embarrass myself, because I'm not sure I'll be able to keep my hands off you! And I've got plenty of holiday and lieu time, so when we get near to a concrete date, just let me know.

Well, that's all for now, darling. I'm sending all my love – and think about my offer!

Love and hugs,

Beryl

xxx

When he got the reply, Maguire pursed his lips and inhaled softly. Just a little care now and the biggest, ripest plum would fall off the tree right into his lap. He must be careful not to be seen to be shaking the money tree. He also had to construct a small chain of accounts through which the money would pass, via a series of non-return valves, until it was untraceable. Anyway, financial confidentiality and client protection would shield him. And, actually, experience showed that sometimes the targets were too humiliated and embarrassed (and usually heartbroken) to involve the authorities. So, a nice clean kill. But the next couple of moves were crucial and speed was of the essence while it was all running hot.

Shortly after the last email, the phone rang. It was Beryl, hoping that she hadn't offended him. He played along. Of course not, but it was a big decision. There was zero risk, but it was her mother's legacy and so she needed to think long and hard about it. The upside for both of them though, he reminded her, was that this could be the opportunity of a lifetime. He promised to think about it. A few hours later he wrote:

Darling,

I think you're right. You've persuaded me. Let's go for it. This is too good a chance to miss. I'll give you a name, sort code, account number, password and ID, and you'll be able to wire the money across. It's in an Escrow account, which means it's quite separate and you'll get written confirmation from the bank on receipt.

I've spoken to the client in principle, who has agreed that if I can find the cash, I will get a fourth share of any profits. He thinks it will be fairly modest, but I've got significant reserves in my budget and savings on subcontracts that are going to rip the top out of it. But we have to be quick. He's given me forty-eight hours max, before he puts it to other potential investors.

Thank you so much for your support and backing in every way. This will be some reward for the tough eighteen months out here and it gives us the opportunity to start our future. Anyway, for security and confidentiality reasons, I will text you all the numbers. Then all you have to do is to tell your bank to press the button.

Let's keep our nerve and we can celebrate with a bottle of Champagne in The Angler in October.

What a year! First meeting the love of my life and now about to get a lottery win to secure our future!

All my love,

Chris

x

Half a day later, Beryl came back to him:

Darling Chris,

So excited about the deal! My hunky man making me a wealthy woman. But I've run into a slight snagette. I went to Hedderwick & Davis, the lawyers who helped me to do the probate on Mum's estate. The money's all there, sitting in an account. But they tell me they can't release it until we pay the Inland Revenue – some stupid rules, apparently. It's only £18,473. Something to do with capital gains, estate duty, unpaid tax, blah-blah-blah. So for the sake of that we might not be able to do the deal in time.

It doesn't sound much, particularly when Mum's estate comes to nearly half a million pounds. It will get sorted eventually and I can pay off my mortgage, etc. But he says it's going to be about six weeks before it is all sorted and the Revenue issue some certificate of release. Then they can pay the funds over.

He said I could just sign a cheque to the Revenue, but all my other savings are tied up in gilts and fixed deposits, which will also take too long to unravel; and my current account I just use for month-to-month costs from my salary.

I'm so angry! I'm really sorry, darling, to let you down at this late stage. I've tried my best, but there is a big conspiracy of lawyers, taxmen, bankers and the like who just want to hang on to our money until we have to jump through hoops for it.

Oh well, I guess it was too good a dream to come true. Please forgive me. I did try. But at least we still have each other.

Love Beryl

x

This email threw Maguire. Damn, damn and double damn the bureaucrats and their crazy, pointless rules. Nothing is *ever* straightforward. Anyway, time for a cool head. His mind raced through all the possible permutations. There *must* be a solution.

After some deliberation, he had it. Unconventional, but a copper-bottomed solution:

Darling Beryl,

I'm so annoyed for you and for us. Just one brief chance to change our lives and the dratted system is conspiring to thwart us.

But there may be a way out of it. If I wire you enough money just to allow you to give a cheque to your lawyer for the Revenue, then they can release the funds in time to beat the deadline, I'm sure. Give me your bank details and I'll get it transmitted electronically. I can pay the fee to make sure it's instant. I've got a bit of spare cash because of all the back pay that was frozen.

We can still do this! Courage, darling; we're nearly there! And we're both in this together!

Maguire wired the money and waited for confirmation. Nothing. He rang Beryl's mobile. No answer. He typed a slightly exasperated email. No reply.

After another forty-eight hours he sat in his bedsit in Birkenhead and pondered. A little light went on in his head.

Meanwhile, Rasheed cleared the £18,473 balance as soon as it hit and then closed the account.

Sitting in the hired one-room office in Peckham, he high-fived his co-conspirator, Madeleine. She thought she made a very convincing Beryl.

Face Time

I can tell people's personalities. Just by looking at their face.

The Greeks had a word for it: personology. Which means that everyone's character is reflected in all the little eddies, lumps, bones, features and lines that we show the world. It's obvious if you think about it a while. Women with thin lips clamped together that you couldn't open with a knife: mean, nasty, tight-assed bitches who wouldn't give you the time of day, so forget about a tip.

Some guys have goofy overbite and jug ears. You just know they're big farm boys with not much happening up there.

I see them all through this little square hatch I put the meals through. Prominent nose: stubborn. Brow overhang: prone to bad temper. Watch out for those guys. Big, wet lips on a woman: a bit too free with her favours.

Yessir! Got them all worked out and never wrong. If I get talking to people when old man McFadyean has too many waitresses off sick and I have to clear, then it always falls into place. I'm always spot on.

Can't recall when I first knew I had this talent. Maybe when that mean sonofabitch who came to stay with Mom was around. Hated him the first time I ever saw him. Before he'd even spoken to me, even I saw bad things in his face. Eyebrows joined up and mouth in that dog snarl all the time. He got what he deserved in the end.

So personology became my personal pet theory when I majored in Psych at Stanford. Oh, I know those academic types don't go for it. A bit too interested in Skinner's rat and Pavlov's dog to understand about people. And I guess they knew I was right and was challenging all their respectable theories. No. It wasn't the "incident" that got me thrown out. It was them protecting their precious turf. Didn't want to let in a new radical who could tell you in a minute what it took them three hours of yammering and tests and questions to discover about people.

Saw lots of interesting faces in the pokey, too. Most of those guys you could predict would end up behind bars. There's just a face that goes with a criminal. Juries can always spot it. Just look at all those pictures in the paper of people who get sent down. You can just tell. Oh, I grant you, it's a bit trickier with clever fraudsters and conmen. Sometimes they can look nearly normal, like you and me, and you have to look very closely to be able to spot the signs.

Yeah. I can read the newspaper, even, and say what they've done from their picture. Just about 100 per cent hit rate. Murderer, rapist, bigamist, thief, accident victim, lottery winner, hero, even those now deceased. Don't ask me how I do it. It's a gift.

You try it tomorrow on the news. You might get some right.

So, you could ask, what am I doing here in the Broadway Diner in some one-horse shithole, knocking up short-order meals? Let's just say that whatever your talents, whatever your gift, when you get a record there ain't much else available to you. I might have a brain and this unique talent, but here I am, sweating twelve hours a day peeling potatoes, flipping eggs, chopping ribs, emptying the swill, cleaning dishes – and all for fifteen bucks an hour.

I should really be a counsellor, a teacher, maybe a cop, using what God gave me to help people; 'cept some of them ain't worth a thought. And they don't like these face tattoos I got to hide my own character.

And you know what? I can see further. I don't just know what they're like – I can see what's happening in their lives, too. Hard to believe, but let me tell you.

Simple case first. That fat guy who comes in with the weak chin and the shifty eyes? Works in the tyre depot. Always a double cheeseburger and fries, with the chocolate cake to follow, no cream. Regular coffee. I could tell before it happened that there were troubles in his marriage. So it was no surprise to me when he snapped about all her bitching and beat her up. You could see that you could just drive him so far then no more. She just didn't understand where that point was. She came in once to chase him out and I could see where it was all going.

How about that tall, thin, old grey-haired guy with deep lines down his face? Just sits there and takes lots of black coffee, staring out the window. Suicide case if I ever saw one. Sure enough, when the bailiffs came to his chicken farm, they found him hanging from a beam in his shed, with all those chickens just pecking round his feet. Pity. Nice quiet guy; never done nothing bad to no one. But I could see where it was all going to end. Should have said something, I guess, but how do you open up on a thing like that?

So you see, I can go that extra step. I can get a fix on their character and I can see what's happening in their lives. But I can also tell pretty much what's *going* to happen to them. Let's say, I'm nearly 100 per cent on the first and second, and about evens on the future. But I'm working on it. I guess you'd call it extrasensory perception or something; except it's all based in science, looking at the face, working out what they're like, then extrapolating – hey! Better not use a word like that or old McFadyean will fall off his cashier stool.

So, if I can predict what's going to happen – and here's the sixty-four thousand dollar question – can I change it? You might be interested to know that, as a scientist, a personologist, it is important to test your hypothesis. I've got a couple of people I'm working on just now.

Case number one is that librarian girl. You might know the type and even you might be able to tell me something about her. Small, thin face with scared eyes. She'll only look at me for a second, when I make a point of taking her chow out. You can guess what she eats: cheese salad; sometimes a vegetarian pizza; glass of milk. No man in her life; never has been. She'd run like a scared rabbit if someone so much as suggests a beer.

But she wants a strong man to take her. That's what she thinks about in bed at night. Gets her off to sleep. That way, she could avoid all that scary dating stuff and small talk. And if he takes her forcefully, then she can pretend she had no choice but to submit and she gets to enjoy it all at the same time. Yes, that's her future. You could call it a form of liberation. Some women just don't know that yet, that's all.

But I'm just as serious about case number two. Big, heavy guy who knocks up fencing on farms round here. Slams his pickup into the car lot, comes in here scattering chairs, with those dog teeth showing. Takes about half a dozen beers with bourbon chasers. He never eats. Never leaves a tip and scares all the waitresses with that big, angry red face. I know that he still lives at home. And you know what? He just terrorises the hell out of his little, old mother. She cooks for him and feeds him. She washes his clothes; fetches and carries. But that bastard doesn't so much as lift a finger.

In fact, I'll tell you, it's worse than that. When he has a drink in him, he'll strike her. What sort of a guy does that to a little old woman? I'll tell you. A disrespectful cockroach that isn't fit to be allowed to carry on getting away with it. He needs stamping on, like those roaches in the kitchen. He shouldn't be on this earth.

So, with this gift of mine comes a responsibility; and it kind of blends. You know what needs to happen and you know what's going to happen. But you want to make it happen, as well. So that's why I'm keeping this record, so people will know why and that I've got good reasons.

First, the librarian. Such a timid, sweet little thing. I know where she lives. This ain't a big town. And I know she's on her own. I'm going to call in there one night. She'll recognise me OK and I'll say I got something with me she dropped from her purse in the diner. Sure, she'll be a bit scared, but we're talking about changing her life for the better. I don't want to be her boyfriend. I just want to help her out a little.

And what about the roach? I sure got something for him. I know where he drinks at night. Seen his pickup parked there. He's always last to go. He keeps that big fourteen-pound persuader in the back of that truck. He won't feel anything. And I've got the keys to the diner. Nobody knows how to use those old meat cleavers like me. He's a big, old slab of meat, but I've got a plan, using the freezer and the swill bin. Shouldn't take more than a week to clear him out. Nobody will know and we'll all be better off.

It's all in the face, you see.

Footnote

'Well, £3,000 is a lot of money in this day and age,' his mother had said, with an admonitory look. 'You mustn't go wasting it. You could get a very acceptable semi-detached here in Dulwich, or maybe invest in shares in your father's company. Or just pop it into the building society for a nice little income.'

He remembered his Aunt Eva's words when she sidled up to him at wicked Uncle Horace's third wedding.

'*Entre nous*, Dominic, although I'm not thinking of cashing in my chips just yet, I've left my favourite nephew a little something in my will,' she wheezed, in a cloud of Cointreau and Woodbines, her favoured combination of vices. 'Whatever you do, don't use it for anything sensible. I'd like to think that you would squander it in fornication, drink and general dissipation – just like I should have when I had the chance!' she laughed.

Later, after Aunt Eva had finally left the croupier and sauntered over to the cashier, he vowed not to let her down. This was, after all, 1962, and the world was opening up to a youthful Cambridge graduate with a tidy sum. Law; politics; banking. The world was young and he could achieve anything. He would leave his footprints.

Yet, what really impelled him was the hunger to write the definitive novel of the late twentieth century. Not one of those gritty northern potboilers which had become so fashionable lately, but – he thought – so evanescent. No, it would be in the great tradition of literature, passing the baton down over the centuries. Homer, Virgil, Dante, Shakespeare, Hugo, Tolstoy, Hemingway. When you are young, you are allowed to dream dreams. Nothing is sensible; all is possible.

And where better to craft his masterpiece than Florence. He remembered a quote from his Classics' tutor that Florence was: "*Fucina di sogni e di passioni*" – a forge of dreams and passions.

So here he was, in the Pensione la Scaletta, between the Duomo and the River Arno, drinking Italian red wine and, he hoped, absorbing by osmosis the centuries of culture and art on his path to immortality.

He hoped that his quotient of Sangiovese was in general keeping with Aunt Eva's wishes; although, the definite absence of squandering and a complete blank on fornication was more a result of his sedate Home Counties upbringing.

The rickety train journey via Paris and Milan had furnished him with a few characters and incidents for sketches and anecdotes; but he was sure that the centuries of culture ingrained in the statues, art and music of Florence would inspire him, and the muse would come calling.

He had chosen the Pensione la Scaletta for its centrality and its serenity. Once the residence of a Florentine nobleman, it was now run by a courteous and efficient German couple called the Schreibers. Mr Schreiber was a tall, patrician presence, calm and solicitous, without being deferential. Mrs Schreiber was small and neat, and endlessly smiling. He liked the building with its squat stone base, its courtyard gardens, and its arthritic concertina lift which took him to the top third floor and his vast room.

He overlooked the gardens and the room was furnished with a selection of baroque furniture, including an ornate oak desk. Perfect! He liked the way that fresh flowers and crisp white linen were silently replenished daily by Signora Schreiber. And with only seven rooms, he liked the way breakfast was served to all the residents every morning at 08.00 a.m. sharp in the cool, communal dining room, with its double doors onto the garden.

It was early season, with only a few residents. There was a businessman, who Dominic observed liked to play stressed Italian executive. He fiercely scanned the business pages of his newspaper and finished his coffee hurriedly before he raced off to ... who knows what, in Central Florence.

Apart from him, the only other residents were an English-speaking family; father, mother and coltish teenager daughter, who all seemed fluent in Italian when ordering more bread, cheese, eggs and coffee.

Breakfast was Dominic's time to consult his Baedeker's Florence with its history, maps, facts and hints on sights and culture. He had spent the first day simply walking and acclimatising. But now it was time for a more systematic cultural absorption to spark the fire for his grand *oeuvre*.

'Will you be staying long?' the father of the family politely enquired from the adjoining table.

The businessman had exited in a flurry of papers and the Schreibers had quietly withdrawn, so it seemed natural for there to be an exchange of a few banal pleasantries.

'Maybe a couple of weeks; it all depends on how things go,' said Dominic enigmatically. 'How about yourselves?'

'I'm an academic from McGill University, in Canada,' said the father. 'Professor of Classical Studies. The university must want me out of the way, because they have given me a furlough by way of research. And what better way to research than to do a grand tour taking in Milan, Verona, Venice, Bologna and now Florence. We have three days here, but then move on to Siena, Rome, Naples and Amalfi. It's a tough job, but someone has to do it,' he smiled. 'And what does your stay depend on?' he asked, echoing Dominic's words.

'I'm a writer,' he said, a little diffidently. 'I'm here for research, too. By way of soaking up the Florentine culture and hoping that it will inspire me. Dominic, by the way. Dominic Deeprose.'

The family looked impressed. The daughter looked at him appraisingly and, for the first time, took in a young man of above average build and dark good looks, but now with maybe a Byronic whiff of fascination about him.

The mother asked, 'And have you been published?'

'Well, only articles and poems in *The Cambridge Student* magazine so far,' he admitted, 'but everyone has to start somewhere.' This, with a disarming smile.

Further exchanges revealed that Father was Enzo Sabatello – English but unsurprisingly of Italian extraction. His wife was Leonora, more retiring and less vocal, who chipped in supportively with more family background.

'And this is Xanthe,' said the Professor, indicating his daughter. 'It means "The Golden One", which she was from the minute she was born, weren't you, darling?'

The daughter smiled confidently, with a smile he found slightly unnerving in somebody not yet an adult. Xanthe was at boarding school in Sussex, but had been allowed out for the tour on the basis that it would broaden her knowledge of geography, art and history. Her final exams were the following year, in any case, so the headmistress had agreed that a couple of weeks of culture and travel each side of the Easter holidays were beneficial.

The family left for the day on a guided tour of the Uffizi, whilst Dominic decided to wander or "busk it", as he termed it.

The following day at breakfast their conversation was more animated and friendly, covering their experiences of the previous day and their intentions for the day ahead.

'We're travelling up out of town to a *castello* owned by a former colleague of mine. It's a fine old place, once owned by one of the Medici family. We'll have a quiet, civilised day overlooking Florence and discussing old times.'

Dominic noticed Xanthe shoot him a surreptitious look of mock horror. He noticed how striking she was, with a very pretty face framed by long golden, almost pre-Raphaelite, hair. He smiled back.

'Well, as for me,' he said, 'I think I'm going to people-watch down by the river, look at the gold shops on the Ponte Vecchio and take coffee overlooking the Piazza della Signoria. Then I shall get myself an authentic Italian picnic and wine, which I will eat in the Boboli Gardens in the sunshine. I want to be immersed in the Florentine atmosphere.'

'I wish I was doing that instead of sitting on some terrace while you all natter about dead people,' said Xanthe, in an amusing, faux-rebellious tone.

'Xanthe, darling, you mustn't impose yourself like that. You haven't been invited and I'm sure our friend doesn't want you along annoying him,' commented her mother sternly.

Dominic shook his head. 'Don't worry. I'm not in the least offended. I'd be pleased if you tag along and' – this to the parents – 'I promise to get her back all in one piece in good time for dinner.'

'Well, if you're absolutely sure. I suppose that's all right, Enzo?'

'Of course,' said the Professor with finality. 'That's settled. I'll give her some lira and we'll see you back here at … shall we say, seven?'

The Sabatellos climbed into their taxi and Dominic was left with Xanthe in the cool, panelled, small, reception hall. She was excited by the freedom and glamour of being able to roam randomly around the city with someone nearer her age, for a change. She was animated, friendly, talkative and challenging in the way of educated teenagers, as they negotiated a series of side streets down to the banks of the Arno. She asked him why he thought Florence was likely to inspire him rather than, say, a poet's garret in Grimsby.

'Well, it's the city of Michelangelo, Leonardo, Dante, Botticelli, Galileo, Raphael, Titian, to name but a few. Not to mention my favourite, Petrarch. There is something in the air or frozen in the pictures, operas and statutes. I can feel it in my bones. Something handed down over the centuries. It worked for all those fellows, anyway.'

'Why is it all about men?' she asked provocatively. 'Where were all the women while all these very great men were turning out paintings and statues and books?'

'Well, most great men were inspired by a muse – usually a woman. Someone is driven by a dream or a passion that is so compelling that they have to write or draw or compose. Take Petrarch, for example. When he was twenty-seven, he glimpsed Laura in a church when she was just seventeen.

'Exactly the same age as me!' she squealed.

'I imagine she may have been a little quieter and perhaps somewhat more serene,' he chided smilingly. 'Anyway, although they probably never met again, since Laura was already married by that time, he was so smitten that he wrote the *Canzoniere* – 366 poems of unrequited love.'

'One for each day of the year and a spare for leap year!' she laughed.

'Well, the point is,' said Dominic, unwilling to be deflected from his thesis, 'without women or lovers, requited or unrequited, much of art would never even be conceived. And you have to remember that, in those days, the role of women was very different. But their role was being a muse to an artist.'

'Well, I want to be a muse. I want someone to paint me, or write a poem about me, or do a great sculpture to please me. Although Miss Saunders, our headmistress, says there is no reason now why girls can't be lawyers, or engineers, or make millions in business, or even be in the Cabinet. But it would be just as nice to be immortalised in something.'

Dominic found himself warming to her youthful confidence and exuberance. And, disconcertingly, he liked the way her blue eyes flashed – and her habit of bunching her hair when she made a particularly compelling point.

So engrossed were they in sparring about culture and philosophy that they reached the Piazza della Repubblica almost without noticing. He told her about the Café Giubbe Rossi, the hotbed of the republican movement and the haunt of artists over the years. He explained the difference between a macchiato freddo and a cappuccino senza schiuma, and watched as she demolished a couple of warm cornetti.

As they walked down to the Ponte Vecchio, she joshed him about what a waste of brain power it was that women were consigned to the role of either muse or matriarch. He admired her ability to argue forensically at the same time as watching her conclude a particularly telling point by prettily widening her eyes and pursing her lips.

He watched her distractedly as they wandered through the Pitti Palace. She charmingly harangued him about the pictures and frescoes showing women as Madonna, La Bella or Venus, whereas the men were great philosophers, artists, sculptors or military leaders.

He suggested that, as it was early afternoon, they take a picnic to the Boboli Gardens adjoining the Palace. They found a back street family delicatessen and bought crostini toscani, prosciutto, artichokes, bread, parmesan cheese and a bottle of Cepparello. They sat on a stone bench near the fountains of the moated gardens, talking, eating and drinking as the sun filtered through the trees.

'So, who is your muse, Dominic Deeprose?' she asked.

He flustered. 'Well, it's more of a composite, a generic ideal, no specific person, just –'

She interrupted triumphantly.

'So, there isn't one! Well, you're going to have to find one if you're going to be as great as you say you'll be!'

They sat silently on the bench for a while, alternately swigging from the wine bottle. They listened to the fountains. He put his hand on the stone bench and their fingers inadvertently touched. He could feel a surge of electricity passing through both of them.

After a while, she said, 'I'd like to sit and watch while you write something. I want to see how it starts in your head, flows down your arm into your hand and then through the pen onto the paper. And, if you like, I can be your muse.'

It was late afternoon when they reached the Pensione la Scaletta. They took the lift to his room, and she sprawled on the bed and watched him as he wrote. As the sun lowered in the gardens, she came and stood by him. He felt her presence very close and smelt her fragrance of coffee, mimosa, wine and flowers. Her bare arm touched his. He could hear her breathing.

'Well, I must be getting back. Parents,' she said airily, 'will be here shortly. Can we continue our argument tomorrow? You'll have to convince them that it will be educational for me or I'm going to be packed off to some dreary church to look at stones,' she said conspiratorially.

And with that, she left.

The following day, at breakfast, the sun shone in from the gardens. They discussed the previous day. Xanthe impressed her parents with a list of cultural exhibits. They said that they were going to Lucca 'to see Puccini's house'. Xanthe made the case for another day of independence.

'Well, that all depends on the good will of Dominic,' said Mrs Sabatello, 'and being sure that it was no imposition.'

Dominic agreed that, absolutely, it would be no trouble and he would be happy to have Xanthe along for company.

'And I have to go with Dominic because I am now his official muse!' she said, by way of final emphasis.

There was an exchange of mock long-suffering.

It was another flawlessly bright spring day. They meandered through the cool streets of a waking city: shouting delivery men; the waft of fresh coffee and baking bread; shutters being raised; Italian voices at a traffic stand-off.

She skipped alongside him with a running commentary of observations, philosophising and questions.

'So, why haven't you got your own muse, young Dominic? After all, you're fairly intelligent, you keep telling me you're gifted and – although not quite handsome – you have quite an interesting face,' she challenged.

'Well, there was someone for a while. A girl called Sandra. But she went away to a different university and it all sort of fizzled out. Last I heard of her, she had taken up with some double-barrelled stockbroker-type. Anyway, how about you?'

'Obviously you're not serious,' she responded, wide-eyed. 'The only boys we see at Beauchamp College come over for the annual joint Shakespeare play. I quite liked the look of one boy called Alan. I was Miranda and he was Prospero. But all he could talk about was his batting average, the Beatles and Cuba. Very boring.'

They reached the Mercato Centrale and bought fresh orange juice and spiced panforte cake.

Their conversation became the centrepiece of the day, punctuated by stops at the obligatory sites: the Duomo, the Baptistery, Santa Croce.

They became unguarded and disinhibited, like lovers in the early flush of a relationship. In the Uffizi, she linked his arm as they admired Michelangelo's *David*. He liked that and felt mildly disappointed when she peeled off to look at another piece.

Lunch was taken at the Cantinetta Antonini and they ate rich fish stew over toasted garlic bread, then creamy zuccotto, with several glasses of Vin Santo.

As they walked back to the Pensione, conversation lulled. They touched together to let other pedestrians past, almost reluctant to separate again.

'Well, we must go and see how your magnum opus is progressing,' she said as they slid the metal lift doors and pressed the brass button to set it in motion.

Wordlessly, they walked into his room. She kicked off her shoes and reclined on his bed, half lying, one hand under her chin, surveying him quizzically for an overlong moment.

'Now what are you up to?' he demanded, as if addressing an errant child.

'I'm amusing myself, musing how best I can be your muse,' she laughed. 'Just you carry on with your great works.'

He worked silently for a while, looking out through the open window to the gardens.

Some while later, she said, 'You carry on, maestro. I'm going to cool off. Walking around in that heat has left me dusty and hot.'

She disappeared out of his room.

Around twenty minutes later, he heard the hinges on the door creak and without looking round, and with a private smile, he said, 'You're such a nuisance, Xanthe Sabatello, disturbing my concentration, just as I'm flowing like the Arno in full spate.'

Silently, she stood next to him. Half turning, he saw that she was wrapped in a long white towel. She leaned over to look at the words on the page. A strand of golden hair touched his face. He could hear himself breathing and felt sure that the beating of the pulse in his head must have been audible.

She stood up straight. He heard and felt the towel slide to the floor.

'Well, wasn't that just like Uncle Dom?' said Hattie, with a rueful smile. 'Everything organised to hell. Labelled folders. Alphabetical files. Instructions on what to do about everything from his will to the car insurance. Such a wonderful man. By the way, I thought the eulogy by Sam was so touching, don't you think? I guess if you haven't got a few people who cry at your funeral, then you haven't lived properly.'

'Agreed,' said Bella. 'I'm going to miss him. I suppose we were his surrogate daughters. Well, everything is in regulation order, but I did find this box of what seems to be jottings and scribblings. And in the top I found this envelope, with a letter in it. It seems to be addressed to someone called Xanthe. Never heard of her, have you, Hatt?'

'Never mentioned her, as far as I know. What does it say, anyway?'

'Well, it's quite long; couple of pages with what seems to be a poem at the end.'

'The mysterious old buffer! Read it out, then!'

'It says:

Dear Xanthe,

It was many years ago, but do you remember me talking to you about Petrarch. He wanted to leave some mark that he had lived, breathed, slept, drank and loved.

He said, "It's possible that some word of me may have come to you again, even though this is doubtful. Since an insignificant name from a half-forgotten man will scarcely penetrate far in time or space."

Like him, I met someone briefly many years ago, but who stayed with me for the rest of my life. We laughed about you being my muse. I have to report that you were singularly unsuccessful! After a brief literary excursion, which came to a halt in a snowstorm of rejection letters, I took the line of least resistance, coupled with a heavy prod in the back from my mother. I passed the exams to enter the civil service. I'm confident that my tightly argued paper on Atlantic cod for the Ministry of Agriculture

Fisheries and Food was highly persuasive. But it was not a literary jewel sparkling on the stretched forefinger of all time.

However, your memory, your beauty, your fragrance stayed with me almost tangibly over the years.

I often wondered what happened to you. Did you become a lawyer or a politician? You certainly could argue fiercely enough! Or maybe a mother and a grandmother? But to me you will always be "The Golden One". Frozen in time for those few days in Florence.

Do you remember the Schreibers at the Pensione la Scaletta? I asked them at breakfast the day you left where the Sabatello family were. They told me you had checked out early in a car to catch the train to Siena.

And you left my life. But you never left my heart. That day, I sat in my room and wrote this poem for you. Usually, poetry needs to be chiselled from an idea, just like a sculptor looks at a rough block of marble and sees how he can fashion a figure. But the chiselling only took me minutes. I don't suppose it will resonate down the years in the pantheon of verse. But it comes from deep within me and when I read it, I smile:

La Scaletta

Outside in the courtyard are sunshine-sharp shadows,
Noises of afternoon echo within
To the cool, slow languor of breeze through the shutters
And electrified dances of hands on damp skin.

Now soft and teasingly urgent caressing,
Tongue, lips and skin and the tilt of soft sighs
Pleasure reflected in clouds that are passing
In liquefied mist of the dew on your eyes.

Lightning at sea and staccato of swans' wings,
Shudders of thunderclaps roll round the hills.
Lamplight stilettos by waters are dancing
Then the storm rolls away and the evening is still.

We are here. It is now. You are warm. I am loving,
Our bodies are tangled like bindweed round briar.
Fragmented pleasure, your indolent beauty
Long kissed away on the blush of desire.

Outside in the courtyard the shadows are lengthening.
The orangery flecked by the sun through the trees.
You must leave me in silence, our fingertips touching,
Quietly, breathlessly, evening at ease.

Who can say, who can say, the way of our ending,
As vapour and dust in the blackness above.
Tomorrow we follow the pathways of mortals,
But today, we are angels,
For today, we have loved.

'So, Xanthe, perhaps in your own way and in my amateur scribbling, you were indeed my muse for one scintilla of time.

'And as long as someone, sometime, somewhere is reading this, you will always be a tiny, immortal footnote in history.'

About the Author

With a far-from-conventional background, Lindsay Pritchard is well qualified to write entertainingly and touchingly about the human condition.

Brought up from a very early age in care in Staffordshire, he nevertheless succeeded in negotiating high school and, later, King's College, London University, where he graduated in Law.

Bored by the prospect of a legal career he sidestepped respectable life for a while, working in a number of menial jobs for several years as a gravedigger, labourer, meat porter and crane driver whilst playing premier-level rugby union at weekends.

However marriage, mortgage and children demanded a more regular lifestyle and income, so he forged a career in Human Resources, eventually becoming the HR Director for a major billion-pound international engineering company. Always considering himself "a writer in a suit, temporarily derailed by circumstances", the demands of a career, three children and another degree – a first in Psychology – did not permit the luxury of sitting at a keyboard waiting for the muse to come calling.

Eventually, a downshift in 2011 at last afforded the opportunity to write.

Harlequinade is his first book.

Lindsay lives in Chester and is currently writing his next book of short stories.

The author supports several charities but has chosen to donate 10 per cent of all royalties from this book to "Help For Heroes".

4662427R00080

Printed in Great Britain
by Amazon.co.uk, Ltd.,
Marston Gate.